THE FIVE MASKS OF DR. SCREEM

GOOSEBUMPS HorrorLand™

Also Available from Scholastic Audio Books

#1 REVENGE OF THE LIVING DUMMY

#2 CREEP FROM THE DEEP

#3 MONSTER BLOOD FOR BREAKFAST!

#4 THE SCREAM OF THE HAUNTED MASK

#5 DR. MANIAC VS. ROBBY SCHWARTZ

#6 WHO'S YOUR MUMMY?

#7 MY FRIENDS CALL ME MONSTER

#8 SAY CHEESE—AND DIE SCREAMING!

#9 WELCOME TO CAMP SLITHER

#10 HELP! WE HAVE STRANGE POWERS!

#11 ESCAPE FROM HORRORLAND

#12 THE STREETS OF PANIC PARK

GOOSEBUMPS HORRORLAND BOXED SET #1–4

WELCOME TO HORRORLAND: A SURVIVAL GUIDE

#13 WHEN THE GHOST DOG HOWLS

#14 LITTLE SHOP OF HAMSTERS

#15 HEADS, YOU LOSE!

#16 SPECIAL EDITION: WEIRDO HALLOWEEN

#17 THE WIZARD OF OOZE

#18 SLAPPY NEW YEAR!

#19 THE HORROR AT CHILLER HOUSE

GOOSEBUMPS®
HALL OF HORRORS

#1 CLAWS!

#2 NIGHT OF THE GIANT EVERYTHING

#3 SPECIAL EDITION: THE FIVE MASKS OF DR. SCREEM

SPECIAL EDITION

THE FIVE MASKS OF DR. SCREEM

R.L. STINE

SCHOLASTIC INC.
New York Toronto London Auckland
Sydney Mexico City New Delhi Hong Kong

ISBN: 978-0-545-28936-8

Goosebumps book series created by Parachute Press, Inc.

12 11 10 9 8 7 6 5 4 3 2 1 11 12 13 14 15 16/0

Printed in the U.S.A. 40
First printing, July 2011

WELCOME TO THE HALL OF HORRORS

THERE'S ALWAYS ROOM FOR ONE MORE SCREAM

Greetings. Come in. You've found my old castle, here in the darkest, most hidden part of HorrorLand.

Pay no attention to those screeching bats. They always get excited when someone new arrives. They think it might be *dinnertime*.

Don't look so terrified. The bats won't bother you. The scorpions will keep them away.

Take a seat next to the coffintable over there. Cozy, right?

No, I don't know who is buried in there. I just hope he's *dead*! Ha-ha.

The Hall of Horrors is a place for very special visitors. A place for kids who have stories to tell.

Frightened kids find their way here. Haunted kids. They are eager to tell me their stories. For I am the Listener. I am the Story-Keeper, the keeper of tales.

We have a visitor today. That girl who keeps

twisting and untwisting a strand of her red hair. Yes, she looks tense.

The girl's name is Monica Anderson. She is twelve.

See that Halloween mask on her lap? That mask is the ugliest thing I've ever seen. (Except when I look in the mirror in the morning. Ha-ha. I have to be careful. I have to sneak up on the mirror so it doesn't break.)

My guess is Monica has a Halloween story to tell. "Why did you bring that mask, Monica?" I ask her.

"I didn't bring it. The mask brought *me*."

"Are you saying that mask is *alive*?"

"I'm saying this Halloween was the most terrifying night of my life. My brother, Peter, and I will never go trick-or-treating again."

"Well, start at the beginning, Monica. I am the Story-Keeper. Tell me your story."

Monica squeezes the ugly mask between her hands. "What happened to Peter and me is hard to believe. Are you sure you want to hear it?"

Go ahead, Monica. Don't be afraid. There's Always Room for One More Scream in the Hall of Horrors.

PART ONE

My brother, Peter, tightened the belt around his white karate uniform. "Monica," he said, "if you get more Snickers bars than me, can we trade?"

He didn't wait for me to answer.

"Mom, are we allowed to eat unwrapped candy?" he shouted. Mom was downstairs. How did he expect her to hear him?

He did a little dance and gave me a hard karate chop on the shoulder.

"*Ow.* Stop it, Peter," I groaned. I rubbed my shoulder.

He laughed. "You're such a wimp." He pretended to chop me again. I ducked away.

"Can you get dizzy from eating chocolate?" Peter asked. "Freddy Milner says if you eat enough chocolate, you get so dizzy, you can't walk straight."

"Don't try it tonight," I said.

He staggered around the room till he crashed into the wall. Then he leaped in the air and did a high karate kick.

"Look out!" I screamed. He almost kicked my laptop off the desk.

"Why don't you get out of my room and wait downstairs?" I said.

"Why don't you make me?" he said. He grinned his toothy grin as he raised both fists.

Peter thinks he's cute, but he isn't. For one thing, he's too tall to be cute. He's ten — two years younger than me — but he's nearly a foot taller than I am. He has stringy blond hair and a long, bent nose and funny teeth. He's my brother but let's face facts — he's a beast.

He picked up a postage stamp from my desk. Licked it — and stuck it to my forehead. Then he collapsed laughing on my bed.

"Why did you do that?" I growled.

He shrugged. "Why not?"

Guess you can understand why I spell Peter's name P-A-I-N.

He talks too much. He can't stand still. He's always dancing and chopping and kicking. And he thinks he's funny, but he isn't.

My friends can't stand him.

Some kids take pills to slow them down to normal speed. But my parents make excuses for Peter. They say he's just high energy.

Like I'm some kind of lazy slob. I'm only captain of the gymnastics team and star sprinter of the Hillcrest Middle School track team.

"What kind of costume is that?" Peter asked with a sneer. "A pair of black shorts over purple tights?"

"It's my gymnastics uniform," I said.

He laughed. "You look like a freak."

"Mom!" I shouted down the stairs. "Do I have to take him?"

I heard her footsteps on the stairs. I stepped out into the hall. She stopped halfway up and leaned on the banister.

"Monica, are you still complaining?" She blew back a strand of her curly copper-colored hair.

She and I have the same color hair. Actually, we kind of look like sisters. We're both small and thin. Unlike Peter and Dad, who are both gangly hulks.

I sighed. "I just want to meet up with Caroline and Regina and hang out with them."

"Well, you can't," Mom said. "You have to take Peter trick-or-treating."

I rolled my eyes. "But, Mom, all he does is practice karate on us till we're black-and-blue."

That made Peter laugh. Behind me in my room, he picked up one of my stuffed pandas and gave it some hard chops.

"You girls can defend yourselves," Mom said. "Kick him back."

Peter dropped the panda to the floor. "Huh?"

"Besides, he'll be too busy collecting candy," Mom said. "You know he's a total candy nut. He won't have time to pester you and your friends."

She shouted to Peter. "Am I right?"

"Whatever," Peter replied.

I sighed again. "Okay, let's get it over with," I said.

I returned to my room and pulled a silvery mask over my eyes. Maybe people wouldn't recognize me. The elastic band caught in my hair. As if being with my brother wasn't enough pain.

I turned and saw Peter pull a black mask down over his eyes. It matched the black belt around his uniform. Peter is nowhere near a black belt. But he wears one anyway.

A few seconds later, we stepped out the front door. Peter hopped down the steps and went running to the street.

It was a dark October night. A half-moon hung low over the houses across the street. The wind gusted, making dead leaves swirl in circles in the front yard.

I shivered. Maybe my shorts and tights and sleeveless T-shirt were a mistake. Maybe I needed a jacket.

But as I followed Peter away from the light of

the house into the blue-black darkness, I realized I wasn't shivering from the wind.

Normally, I'm not a fraidy cat. But I just had a feeling . . .

. . . A very bad feeling about this Halloween.

2

Caroline wore a top hat, a man's ragged overcoat, big floppy shoes, and a bumpy rubber nose. She spoke in a high, creaky voice and said she was a Munchkin from *The Wizard of Oz.*

Regina wore gray spandex workout clothes. She had black whiskers painted on her cheeks. She said she was Catwoman. With her olive-colored eyes, she looked like a cat even without the whiskers.

All three of us are on the gymnastics team at school. So we are pretty strong and athletic.

But we were no match for Peter.

He kept dancing around us, making wide circles. Then he'd dart in and snatch something out of our trick-or-treat bags. He was a total thief.

"Give that back!" Regina cried. She made a grab for the candy bar Peter swiped. "That's my favorite!"

"Mine, too," Peter said, dancing away, giggling his head off. He shoved Regina's candy into his big shopping bag.

Regina didn't give up easily. She let out a roar and dove at Peter.

He dodged to the side and gave her a hard karate chop — in the neck.

"*Ullllp.*" Regina made a horrible noise and started to choke.

For once, Peter stopped dancing. "Oh. Sorry," he said. "That was an accident."

"*This* is an accident, too!" Caroline cried. She lowered her shoulder and plowed right into Peter.

The two of them went rolling into a pile of dry leaves. Peter held on to his trick-or-treat bag for dear life. He swung it at Caroline, and she rolled away from him.

Regina rubbed her throat. "I'm okay," she said.

"It was an accident. Really," Peter insisted. He jumped up and trotted over to Regina. He held up his shopping bag. "Take a candy. Go ahead. Take any one."

Regina eyed him suspiciously.

He shook the bag in front of her. She reached in and pulled out a big Snickers bar.

"Not *that* one!" Peter cried. He grabbed it out of her hand and backed away with it.

Regina let out a groan. "You creep!"

Caroline took Regina by the arm and started to pull her away. "Catch you later, Monica," she called.

"Hey, wait —" I started after them. "Where are you going?"

"Away from the Karate Monster," Caroline said. "*Far* away."

My two friends took off, running hand in hand down the sidewalk. I watched them appear and disappear in the circles of light from the streetlamps.

Then I turned angrily to my brother. "Thanks for chasing my friends away," I snapped.

He shrugged. "Can I help it if they're losers?"

I wanted to punch his lights out. But we're a nonviolent family. I mean, everyone but Peter.

So I just swung my fists in the air and counted to ten.

"Okay." I felt a little less angry. "Let's go home." I started to walk, but Peter grabbed my shoulder and spun me around.

"We can't go home, Monica. It's too early. And look —" He shook his big shopping bag so I could hear the candy rattling around inside it. "My bag is only half full."

I laughed. "You're kidding, right? You really think you're going to fill that *huge* bag? No way. That would take all night."

"Okay, okay," Peter replied. "Just one more block. Two more blocks. Three —"

I rolled my eyes. "One more block, Peter. But you can do both sides of the street."

"Okay. Stand back. Here goes." He ran full speed up the front lawn to a brightly lit house with a big grinning jack-o'-lantern in the front window. A flickering candle inside it made its jagged eyes glow.

I stayed at the curb and watched him ring the doorbell. A girl in a Dora the Explorer costume appeared at the door.

Shivering, I hugged myself. The wind had grown colder. It felt heavy and damp, as if it might snow. The half-moon had disappeared behind dark clouds.

It was getting late. I glanced up and down the street. I didn't see any other trick-or-treaters. Peter is such a candy freak. I knew he'd stay out all night if he could.

But I wanted to get home and warm up. And call Regina and Caroline and apologize for Peter for the ten thousandth time this month.

I stayed down by the curb and watched him run from house to house. This was his biggest night of the year. Bigger than Christmas.

When he got home, he'd turn the shopping bag over on his rug and dump out all the candy. Then he'd sort it for hours, making piles of this candy bar and then another.

He's so totally mental. Sometimes when he was smaller he'd actually roll on his back in his Halloween candy, like a dog.

Of course, that was when he was still cute. Now he only *thinks* he's cute.

I watched him run up to the last house on the block. It was a tiny square house with two bikes lying on their sides in the front yard. A young woman answered the door and started to hand Peter an apple.

"No way!" he cried. "No apples!" He spun away before she could drop it in his bag. Then he leaped off her front stoop and came running toward me.

"Monica, we have to do one more block," he said breathlessly.

I crossed my arms in front of me. "Peter, you promised," I said. "One last block. That was it."

"But — but —" he sputtered. "Did you see what happened up there? She tried to give me an *apple*! No candy."

I rolled my eyes. "Big tragedy," I said.

"Come on, Monica. Give me a break." He started to pull me across the street.

"It's late," I said. "Mom and Dad will be worried. Do you see anyone else still out here?"

He didn't answer. He tore across the street and started to run along a tall hedge at the corner.

"Peter? Come back here!" I called after him.

But he disappeared into the deep shadow of the hedge.

Where were we? I couldn't read the street sign. The streetlight was really dim. Without any moonlight, it was too dark to see anything.

Tall hedges rose up like black walls. Behind them, high trees whispered and shook.

We never go this far, I told myself. *I don't know this block.*

As my eyes adjusted to the darkness, houses came into focus. Big houses on top of steep, sloping lawns. No lights in the windows. No one moving. No cars on the street.

A sudden howl made my skin prickle.

Was that a cat? Or just the strong wind through the old trees?

I realized my heart was suddenly thudding in my chest. I turned and chased after Peter.

He was halfway up a long driveway that led to an enormous house nearly hidden behind hedges and tall shrubs. The house looked like an old castle, with pointed towers on both sides.

"Peter?" My voice came out in a hoarse whisper.

I trotted to catch up to him. "Let's go home," I said. "This house is totally dark. The *whole block* is totally dark. We've wandered into a weird neighborhood."

He laughed. "You're afraid? Ha-ha. Look at you. Shaking like a baby."

"I — I'm not afraid. But it's creepy," I said. "Let's go. Now. No one is going to answer the door here."

He adjusted the belt on his karate uniform. Then he straightened the black mask over his eyes. "Let's see," he said.

He pushed the doorbell. I could hear loud chimes inside the house.

Silence.

"See? No one's coming," I said. "Come on, Peter. I'm freezing. And you have plenty of candy. Let's go home."

He ignored me, as usual. He pushed the doorbell again and held it in.

Again, I heard the chimes on the other side of the tall wooden door.

The trees shook in a strong wind gust. Dead leaves blew up against the front stoop, as if trying to get to us.

I heard another howl. Far away. It sounded almost human.

"Peter, please —" I whispered.

And then I heard footsteps. A clicking sound inside the house.

The door squeaked and then slowly slid open. A dark-haired woman in a long dress peered out at us.

Gray light shone behind her. I couldn't see her face clearly. It was hidden in shadow.

"Trick or treat," Peter said.

The woman took a step toward us. I could see her dark eyes go wide.

"Oh, thank goodness!" she cried. "You're here. I *knew* you would come!"

She pulled us into her house. I blinked in the shimmering gray light.

We stood in a narrow front entryway. The ceiling was high above our heads. The light came from a huge glass ball dangling on a thick chain above us.

"We — we're just trick-or-treating," Peter stammered.

The woman nodded. Her straight black hair fell over her face. She brushed it back with a pale hand.

I couldn't tell how old she was. Maybe in her thirties, like our parents.

She was pretty, with round, dark eyes, high cheekbones, and a warm smile. Her black dress fell to her ankles, soft and flowy like a nightgown.

"I knew you would come," she repeated.

"What do you mean?" I asked.

She didn't answer. She turned quickly, her

long dress swirling around her. And led the way into an enormous, dimly lit front room.

A low fire flickered in a wide stone fireplace on the far wall. It sent long shadows dancing into the room.

Antique black leather couches and armchairs filled the big room.

A tall painting hung over the mantel. It was a portrait of a sad-looking woman in old-fashioned lacy clothes, a single teardrop on one cheek.

Despite the fire, the room was cold. The air felt damp and heavy.

What a totally depressing place, I thought. *Everything is so dark and creepy.*

"My name is Bella," the woman said. She tossed her hair off her forehead with a snap of her head. She stood facing us with her hands at her waist. Her dark eyes moved from Peter to me.

"You are Monica, aren't you?" she said. "And your brother is named Peter."

I felt my throat tighten. "How did you know?" I asked.

"Who are you?" Peter demanded. "Do you know our parents or something?"

She shook her head. A thin smile spread over her pale, slender face. "You're in the book," she said softly. Her eyes stayed locked on us, as if studying us.

"Book?" I said. "I don't understand."

She leaned a hand against the back of one of the big armchairs. "The book says you would come. It says you will help me tonight."

I glanced at Peter. He rolled his eyes.

Is this woman crazy? I thought.

"We're in a book?" I asked. "You mean, like a phone book?"

Bella shook her head. She motioned for us to follow her. She led us to a library at the back of the living room.

Bookshelves climbed to the ceiling on all four walls. The shelves were filled with old-looking books. The covers were cracked and faded.

Two lamps that looked like torches poked out from high on the walls. The lamps threw yellow light over a long wooden table. Four straight-backed chairs stood around the table.

Blue-black shadows stretched everywhere. I shivered. I had the strange thought that the shadows were *alive*.

Bella reached down to a lower shelf and tugged out a large book. She raised it in both hands and blew dust off the cover.

As she brought it to the table, I saw that the cover was cracked and stained. She held it up so that Peter and I could read the title etched in curly brown letters on the front: *The Hallows Book*.

"Hallows?" I said. "It's . . . like a Halloween book?"

She didn't answer. With a groan, she set the heavy book down on the table. Then she leaned over it, turning the yellowed pages carefully.

"I . . . don't understand," I said. "What is this book?"

"We just came for candy," Peter said. His voice trembled. I could see he didn't like this.

"Read," Bella said. She ran a slender finger down a page. "Come closer, you two. Read what the book says."

Peter and I leaned over the book. It smelled kind of musty, like the closets at Grandma Alice's house. I squinted at the tiny, faded type, and read:

On Halloween night, the doorbell will ring. Two young people will come to Bella's aid. Their names will be Monica and Peter Anderson.

They will be celebrating the rituals of All Hallows' Eve. But Peter and Monica will give up their celebrations. And they will help Bella in her time of need.

I tried to swallow. My throat suddenly felt dry as cotton.

Peter and I stared down at the faded page of the old book. The writing ended there. The rest of the page was blank.

I raised my eyes to Bella.

"This is impossible," I said. "How can this be?"

"It is written in the book," Bella said. Her dark eyes glowed. "So it must be true."

I grabbed Peter by the arm. "Let's go," I said. "This is too weird."

"You can't!" Bella cried. She moved quickly and blocked the doorway to the library.

Peter and I almost ran right into her. She spread her arms to keep us from sliding past her.

"You can't keep us here!" Peter cried.

"*The Hallows Book* says you will stay," Bella said. Her dark eyes flashed again. She gazed past us to the open book on the table. "You won't leave. The book says you won't leave."

"I — I don't know how you did that book trick," I said. "But really. You have to let us go home. Why do you need our help anyway?"

Bella pointed to the old book. "It says you will stay and help me. The five masks — they will be stolen, as they are every year. You will help me get them back."

"Five masks?" I cried.

"I know karate," Peter blurted out. He raised a hand, as if he was going to give Bella a chop. "Better let us go."

Her eyes went wide. "Peter, I'm not going to hurt you," she said. "I'm not trying to hold you prisoner. *The Hallows Book* says that you will help me get back the masks."

Peter lowered his hand. "I get it," he said. He shook his head. "It's Halloween, and you like to give kids a good scare on Halloween. It's a big joke, right?"

Bella moved to the table. "The book isn't a joke. It tells everything that happens."

"What five masks are you talking about?" I asked. "Are they Halloween masks?"

"They are called the Masks of Screem. They are masks of powerful magic," Bella said.

Peter and I exchanged glances. She was definitely a nut job.

Should we run while we had the chance?

I leaned down and gazed at the open book. To my surprise, I saw new writing on the page. A new paragraph had appeared. I read it to Peter. . . .

"Peter and Monica didn't trust Bella. They couldn't decide what she wanted of them. At

first, they believed her to be insane. The two youngsters wanted to run.

"But they had an important mission to accomplish. Bella desperately needed their help. In fact, the whole world needed their help.

"They could not run."

"Too weird," Peter said, shaking his head. He tugged off his black mask and let it fall to the floor. He wiped sweat off his face with the back of his hand.

"Definitely too weird," I murmured.

"Let me show you the five masks," Bella said. "They are mine now. But not for long."

She led us to one wall of bookshelves. She reached for a red-covered book and pulled it from its shelf.

A few seconds later, I heard a humming sound. The whole shelf began to spin. As the shelf turned, the books disappeared. And a hidden compartment in the wall came into view.

Hanging in the compartment were five Halloween masks.

I uttered a gasp. The masks were ugly and frightening.

I recognized a skull . . . a mummy head . . . a hideous wolf head, its fangs bared in a silent snarl. . . .

"Whoa. Those are majorly *scary*!" Peter exclaimed.

"You don't know what you are saying," Bella

replied in a whisper. "You don't know the meaning of *scary*."

She motioned us closer. "Come here. Don't stand back there. Take a good look at them."

Peter stepped up. His eyes were on a furry pig-face mask with curled yellow horns poking out of the top.

I held back. My skin was prickling again. I felt cold all over.

True fear. Just *looking* at the masks was frightening.

And then . . . then . . . as I stared in fright . . .

. . . The mouths on all five masks dropped open — and they began to howl.

5

I couldn't hold it in. I opened my mouth in a shrill scream.

Peter and I staggered back. I wanted to get as far away from those howling masks as I could.

We started for the door — and tripped over each other.

Peter sailed to the floor and landed hard on his side. I caught my balance and reached down to help him up.

The masks' howls faded. The ugly mouths closed again. But I could still hear the frightening sound in my mind.

Peter fixed the belt on his karate uniform. We both edged toward the library door.

"I'm sorry," Bella said softly. "But you do have reason to be afraid."

"I don't want to hear any more," I said. "Just let us go home."

"I need to explain," Bella said, tossing back

her long hair. "You must know everything if you are to help me."

"No. Really —" I started. "Peter and I —"

"I have been guarding these evil masks for one hundred years," Bella said.

"Yeah. Sure," Peter muttered. "You look younger than our mother."

"Just let us go," I insisted.

She had to be a *lunatic.*

"There is magic involved," Bella said. "I am one hundred and thirty years old."

"And I'm SpongeBob SquarePants," Peter said.

Bella's pale face darkened in anger. She stared hard at Peter. "I am not insane," she said. "If you want to get home safely, you need to listen to me — and believe. At least give me a chance."

IF we want to get home?

Was that a threat?

Bella's words sent a chill down my back.

I crossed my arms tightly in front of me. "Go ahead," I said. "We won't interrupt."

Bella motioned to the masks hanging limply in the shelf. "These masks were made one hundred years ago," she said. "They were created by a powerful sorcerer. His name was Hallows."

"He wrote that book?" Peter asked, pointing to the book on the table.

Bella nodded. "Hallows was born on a Halloween night," she continued. "Many years later, he died on a Halloween night. After he made these masks, he gave them strong magic. Magic that comes to life only one night a year — tonight."

I stared at the masks. "Tonight . . ." I murmured.

"Hallows gave the masks to the evil Dr. Screem," Bella said. "That's why they are called the Masks of Screem. But I cannot let him keep the masks. His evil is too great."

I took a deep breath to work up my courage. "I've heard enough," I said. "Peter and I are leaving."

"It's a good scary story," Peter told Bella. "Maybe you should make a movie of it or something."

Bella stared at us both. She didn't reply. She raised her hands to the sides of her face.

Peter and I started to back away from her. I took a final glance at the ugly masks. They hung limply on their hooks and didn't move.

We turned and took two hurried steps toward the library door.

Then we both gasped in horror.

The door was GONE.

My eyes swept the library. Four walls of bookshelves from the floor to the ceiling.

No door.

No door where there *had been a door*!

Panic made my legs tremble. Another chill rolled down my back.

"Where's the door? Let us out!" Peter cried. He began running frantically around the room, pushing on the shelves. Trying to find a way out.

"Be calm," Bella said, nearly in a whisper. "Don't you see? Once you are in, the way out is difficult. Your journey has just begun. There's no turning back."

"We don't want to go on a journey," I said. My voice shook, revealing my panic. "We just want out of here."

Peter shoved his shoulder against a shelf. It didn't budge.

"You can't keep us prisoner here," I said. "Our parents —"

"You're not prisoners," Bella said. "You have come to help me — remember?"

"You're crazy!" Peter screamed. "Let us out of this room!"

"I am not your enemy," Bella told him. "Come. Sit down. Relax. I need your help. I swear I'm not going to hurt you."

She shoved the red book back into its shelf. The masks disappeared as the shelf turned around. "Properly hidden," she murmured.

Then she moved to the table in the center of the room and pulled out two chairs. "Come, you two. Sit down. Please."

Peter and I glanced at each other. We knew we didn't have a choice.

Maybe if we let Bella finish her story, she would let us go.

We dropped down onto the chairs and slid them up to the table. Bella sat across from us. Her fingers tapped the tabletop. Her fingernails were long, painted dark red. "May I continue?"

Peter and I stared back at her in silence.

"I was telling you about the sorcerer named Hallows," Bella said. "Hallows made the five masks. He filled them with powerful magic. He gave them to Screem. He didn't know of Screem's evil. Then Hallows created this book. He named it *The Hallows Book*."

I lowered my eyes to the book. My mind spun. I was trying to figure out how Bella got our names in that book.

But I didn't have a clue.

"Screem is my enemy," Bella said. "I struggle every year to keep the masks from him. But every year, he steals them. Every Halloween, we must struggle over the masks. He steals them and hides them, but they must be found!"

I felt a shiver of fear as Bella stared into my eyes and said:

"The hunt for the five masks has been going on every Halloween night for one hundred years. And I am forced to play the same dangerous game year after year."

"So . . . you really are one hundred and thirty years old?" I cried.

She raised a hand to silence me.

"Screem is all evil," she said. "His evil is beyond anything we know. I cannot allow him to keep the masks."

Her voice faded. She shut her eyes for a long moment.

Then she said, "If I don't keep the masks away from him, the world will be in terrible danger."

"Okay," I said. "You have the masks safely hidden away here. Can we go now?" I scooted my chair back.

"You don't understand!" Bella cried, raising her voice for the first time. She jumped to her feet. "Screem will steal them. Every year, our story repeats. Every year, he steals them back from me and hides them in different places. If you leave, how will I get them back? I can't go after them."

"I . . . don't understand," I said. My head was spinning.

Did *any* of this make sense?

"I can't go after the masks," Bella said. "When Screem steals them, I need someone else to hunt them down. Someone to help me. That's why you're here."

Her dark eyes glistened with tears. "The sorcerer Hallows made the rules of the hunt. He put a curse on me. If I touch any of the masks, I will crumble to ashes."

Peter rolled his eyes. Her story got crazier and crazier.

Why was I starting to believe her? Maybe it was the tears that were brimming in her eyes. Maybe it was the desperate tremble of her soft voice.

"Every Halloween night, I must find someone to help me," Bella continued. "When Screem steals the masks, I need someone to go on the hunt and collect them. Someone to bring them back to me. This year, you two are the ones to risk your lives."

"If you're trying to give us a Halloween scare, it's working," Peter said. He stood up. "We listened to your story. Now let us go home."

"I can't let you go home," Bella said. "I am helpless against Screem. I cannot use magic against him. I have no powers that can stop him."

She slid the heavy old book across the table. "Look at it. Read what it says. The book doesn't lie. The book says you will be the ones to help me this year."

Peter and I leaned over the book. We ran our eyes down the tiny type. A new paragraph had appeared.

It said pretty much what Bella had just told us. It named Peter and me. It said we had come to help her. . . .

They didn't believe Bella's story. They didn't believe that the Halloween mask hunt was real. They were eager to escape the old mansion and return home.

But the story of the old sorcerer Hallows and the Five Masks of Screem was true. This year, it was Peter and Monica's turn to meet the challenge. And perhaps . . . save the world from untold evil.

And then the last words caught my eye.

The last words . . . I read them twice. I felt my

heart start to pound. I had that trembling feeling in my legs again.

I read the last words out loud:

"Monica and Peter were frightened by Bella's story. But their true terror wouldn't start FOR ANOTHER FIVE MINUTES."

The book ended there. I stared at the final sentence.

"What does that *mean*?" I cried.

Bella didn't answer. Her eyes burned into mine.

"It means we have five minutes to get *out* of here!" Peter cried.

We both jumped up.

"You *have* to let us go," I told Bella. "Peter and I can't help you."

Before Bella could reply, a loud crash made Peter and me cry out in surprise.

I swung around — and saw books sliding off the high shelves, tumbling to the floor. Peter and I ducked under the table as heavy old books flew across the room.

Earthquake, I thought.

I covered my head and shut my eyes.

Books crashed and thudded all around me.

Books bounced off the tabletop, over the floor. It was *raining* books!

And then — another crash. My eyes shot open in time to see a whole wall collapse.

No. Not a wall. A bookshelf fell over. It slammed to the floor with a deafening crash. The room shook. A curtain of dust floated up into the air.

Then silence.

I picked up my head — and watched a man stride into the library from behind the fallen bookcase. He wore a long purple robe with a purple hood. He had a red face and a square white beard that looked like a paintbrush.

He came stomping over the books, kicking them out of his way. He was short, I noticed. He was no taller than Peter.

He stared hard at Peter and me as he stormed into the room. He had purple eyes that glowed like jewels.

"Dr. Screem!" Bella cried, raising her hands to her face. "Keep back. Keep back!"

He stared straight ahead as if he didn't hear her.

"Dr. Screem — please!" Bella pleaded. "Stay away from them! Don't *hurt* them!"

But Screem kept up his march over the fallen books. He strode straight toward my brother and me.

And the look on his bearded face was *not* friendly.

"Don't touch them! Don't hurt them!" Bella screamed.

I froze in terror for a long moment. Then I grabbed Peter and pulled him backward till we bumped against a shelf.

Screem marched straight ahead.

I held my breath until my chest hurt. My knees felt like they were about to collapse. I leaned back against the bookshelf to keep from falling.

"No — please!" Bella cried, hands pressed to her face.

But Screem didn't have his purple eyes on us. He was gazing straight ahead at the hidden compartment holding the five masks.

Bella gasped. "No! Stay away!" She moved quickly. She dove to the shelf and tried to block it with her body.

Screem pointed a finger at her. I saw a big green ring on his finger.

I gasped as a beam of green light shot out

from the ring. The light swept over the bookshelf.

It began to turn. In seconds, the five masks were revealed.

Screem advanced. Bella backed away in fright. He reached inside and snatched the five masks one by one.

He squeezed them together, cradling them under his arm.

"No! No! No!" Bella cried. She ran at Screem, lowered her shoulder — and tried to tackle him.

But he ducked away. Bella slammed onto the floor and slid on her stomach. Her long hair flew up behind her. She let out a frustrated cry.

Screem hid the masks under his robe. He gazed down at Bella as she climbed slowly to her feet. And a strange smile crossed his bearded face.

"And so it begins again," he said softly. His voice was high and whistly, breathy like an old man's voice.

"Screem, listen to me —" Bella pleaded.

"You cannot stop me. It is written in the book. The hunt begins again," Screem said. "But this time when it is all over, the masks — and all their power — will be mine."

"No —" Bella protested.

"When Halloween ends, your control of the masks will end, too," Screem told Bella.

His purple robe swept around him as he turned and started for the opening near the fallen bookshelf.

Bella took a few steps after him but stopped. I could see her chin trembling, see the fear on her pale face.

At the shelf, Screem spun around. He waved a long finger at Peter and me. "Keep away. I'm warning you," he growled.

I stared at the green ring on his finger. It set off a beam of green light, like laser light.

"Don't try to help her," he cried. "I know who you are."

The library door suddenly rose up in front of him. With another swirl of his robe, he disappeared out the door.

His words rang in my ears.

I know who you are. . . . I know who you are. . . .

Each time I heard them, another chill shook my body.

Bella came striding over to us. She suddenly looked older. She had deep lines under her dark eyes. Her lips were dry and cracked.

"Now you have no choice," she murmured.

I squinted at her. "Excuse me?"

"You have no choice," she repeated. "You *must* help me. Screem knows who you are. That means you are in terrible danger."

Okay. Okay. I'm a very patient person. I can put up with a lot of nonsense.

I'm a calm person. I can deal with difficult people.

I have to put up with Peter, after all.

I think I'm pretty good in an emergency.

But every person has a limit. And I'd just reached mine. I'd had enough.

I took a deep breath and held it. I waited for the chills to stop rolling down my back.

Then I grabbed Peter by the shoulder and gave him a push. "Let's go!" I cried, motioning to the door with my head.

"Stop!" Bella ordered.

"We're out of here!" I said. "You and that little wizard Screem are both crazy."

"Yeah. Happy Halloween!" Peter cried.

And we both took off. We ran right past her. Slipping and sliding on the old books on the floor, we leaped over the fallen bookshelf. And darted through the library doorway.

I heard Bella shouting, but I didn't turn back.

I tugged open the front door of the house, and Peter and I rocketed outside.

The cold night air shocked my hot face. Swirling winds sent my hair flying up.

Our shoes slapped the hard ground as we ran side by side down Bella's front lawn. We practically burst through the tall hedges at the street and kept running.

I glanced back. I expected Bella to be chasing after us.

But the street was empty. Nothing moved. No people in view. No cars.

It must be late, I realized. *No trick-or-treaters on the street.*

Mom and Dad will be furious.

And if we tell them what happened to us . . . they'll say we made it all up.

Peter and I ran down the middle of the street. I ran so hard, I had a sharp pain in my side. But I ignored it and kept running.

We reached the corner of our block. Peter nearly tripped over his trick-or-treat bag.

How could he still be carrying it?

There we were in the scariest moment of our lives. And all he could think of was holding on to his Halloween candy? Amazing.

We ran past the Willers' house. Then the small empty field with the baseball diamond marked in the dirt. Then the Kleins' house.

My legs were aching. The pain in my side was *intense.*

Just a few more steps . . .

And then Peter and I both stopped running. And we both let out screams at the same time.

"NOOOO."

"Oh, NOOOO."

My throat tightened in horror. I struggled to breathe.

I gazed up to the top of the low slope where our house had stood.

It was gone.

Our house was *gone.*

Peter and I were staring at an empty lot.

"Wh-where is it?" Peter stammered. His eyes bulged and his mouth hung open.

We were both panting too hard to speak. I could feel the blood pulsing at my temples. I dropped to my knees to get over my dizziness.

"It's . . . gone," Peter choked out. "But . . . where are Mom and Dad?"

I shook my head. I looked away from him. I didn't want this to be real.

I had the idea that if I looked away, then turned back, our house would be where it always stood.

But no.

Tall grass swayed in the gusting winds all the way up the sloping front. Nothing but tall grass.

"We — we're on the wrong block," I said, still struggling to catch my breath. "That's all. The wrong block."

I climbed to my feet and gazed around. "Come on. This is crazy, Peter. We just got mixed up.

Check the street sign. Our house must be on the next block."

"No," Peter replied in a whisper. "Monica, look."

He pointed to the tree at the top of the lot. The fat maple tree with the low limbs that he and I like to climb.

I let out a long, unhappy sigh. "Yes. That's our tree," I murmured. "You're right."

The tree stood at the end of the stone walk that led to the driveway. But now there was no walk. No driveway.

No house.

My whole body shook. My teeth were chattering. I hugged myself tightly but it didn't help stop the shakes.

I need my parka, I thought.

What a crazy idea. How could I get my parka if my house was gone?

"This can't be happening," Peter said. His voice cracked. "How can a whole house disappear?"

"Dr. Screem," I murmured. "He said he knew who we were. He said he didn't want us to help that crazy woman Bella."

Peter squinted at me. "Do you really think Screem did this? To show us how tough he can be?"

I shrugged. It didn't make any sense to me. I just didn't want to believe it.

“Was Bella telling the truth?” Peter asked. “That whole story about collecting the five masks every year to keep them out of Screem’s hands?”

I didn’t answer Peter. I was thinking hard. I stared at the neighbors’ house, and it gave me an idea.

I pointed to the Kleins’ house. “It’s still there. Like always,” I said.

There were lights on in the front window and in two upstairs windows. Yellow light washed over their front stoop.

“The Kleins must know what happened to Mom and Dad,” I said.

Peter took off, running up the middle of their lawn. I raced after him.

Maybe the Kleins saw something. Maybe they could tell us something that would help us.

They had always been nice neighbors. They were the ones who marked the baseball diamond in the field down the block.

Mrs. Klein was the girls’ basketball coach at my school. Mr. Klein traveled a lot. He always brought new kinds of candy bars home for Peter.

They were younger than our parents. Their daughter, Phoebe, was only in preschool.

My hand was shaking so hard, it took three tries to ring their doorbell. Peter leaned over the stoop and peered into their front window. "I can't see them," he said.

I rang the bell again. I was very eager to talk to them.

Finally, I heard footsteps inside and murmured voices.

The door swung open, and more yellow light spread over the stoop. I blinked a few times — and stared at the old couple standing in the doorway.

He was bald and red faced, and his thick square eyeglasses made his dark eyes bulge like frog eyes.

She had short white hair and a round chubby face. She wore a long flowered dress and leaned on a brown cane.

They both eyed us up and down. "Yes? Can we help you?" the woman said finally.

"Wh-where are the Kleins?" I blurted out.

They glanced at each other. He blinked his big froggy eyes. "The Kleins?"

"This is their house," Peter said.

They both shook their heads. "No. You must have the wrong place. We don't know the Kleins."

"But that's *impossible*!" My voice came out more shrill than I'd planned. But I couldn't keep my panic down. "You *have* to know the Kleins. They've lived here for years."

"Must be some kind of Halloween prank," the woman muttered to her husband.

He started to shut the door. "Sorry. You have the wrong house," he said. "Are you sure you're on the right street?"

"Y-yes," I stammered. My heart pounded so hard, I could barely breathe. "We're on the right street. That was our house next door." I pointed to where our house had stood.

"You know the house next door?" Peter asked. "That was our house. But all of a sudden —"

The old man's face turned cold. "Sorry, kids. I don't really get the joke," he said.

Leaning on her cane, his wife stepped up to the door. "There's *never* been a house next door," she said. "It's *always* been an empty lot."

PART TWO

10

The horror had begun. Just as the old book predicted.

Finding yourself written about in a yellowed old book was scary enough. But finding yourself with nowhere to live . . . with your parents missing and your house vanished . . .

It was almost too horrifying to bear.

Our whole world had turned upside down. I wanted to push a REWIND button and go back to that afternoon, back to when our lives were normal.

Would we ever see our parents again?

Peter shivered in his karate uniform. His trick-or-treat bag stood in the grass beside him. He had both hands shoved deep into his pockets.

I could see he was trying hard not to cry.

Peter never even cried when he was a baby. He was always tough and fearless. Once, he jumped into a friend's swimming pool, and he didn't even know how to swim.

He just wasn't afraid of anything. He splashed around until he started to float. Mom and Dad didn't have to fish him out. I think he was three at the time.

Knowing that, it felt even worse to see him so frightened and upset.

"We have no choice," Peter said.

I turned to him. "You mean we have to go back to Bella's house?"

He nodded. "It might be the only way to get our house back."

So we hurried through the dark, empty streets. I saw lights on in a few houses. But many were dark.

Two cats followed us for a while. They yowled at us as we trotted down the middle of the street. Maybe they were warning us to turn back. My brain was filled with crazy thoughts like that.

The cats lost interest after a block or two and ran behind a house.

As we made our way past the tall hedges in front, we could see all the lights on in Bella's house. The front door was open. She stood in a pool of gray light, as if she was expecting us.

We ran up to her, both panting hard. "Our house . . ." I choked out. "Our house is gone."

"Can you help us?" Peter asked.

She waved us inside and shut the door. We followed her into the front room.

The fire crackled loudly in the fireplace. The flames danced high, sending flickering shadows over the room.

She handed us two glass cups of yellow liquid. "This will warm you up," she said.

I eyed the cup suspiciously. "What is it?"

She frowned at me. "It's hot apple cider," she said. "If you want me to help you, you have to learn to trust me, Monica."

I took a sip. It was sweet and hot and felt good on my dry throat. I took another sip.

"How can we trust you?" I blurted out. "Our house is gone. And our parents. Everything. Gone."

Bella shut her eyes. "It was Screem," she said. She opened them and gazed hard at Peter and me. "I warned you."

"Screem made our house disappear?" Peter asked.

"He wasn't lying — for once," she said. "He *does* know who you are. And he wanted to show you —"

"Show us what?" Peter interrupted.

"Show you how powerful he is," Bella said. "Do you see the evil power he has with those masks? He can change reality. Make houses disappear. Make people disappear — forever."

I gasped. A wave of fear swept over me. "Make them disappear *forever*?" I asked.

Bella nodded. "Forever," she said.

"But . . . h-how can we bring our parents back?" I stammered.

Bella frowned again. Her dark eyes went dull.

"You can't," she said in a whisper.

"Huh?" I uttered a gasp. I felt my heart skip a beat.

"What do you *mean* we can't?" Peter cried. "We *have* to do something. We *have* to bring them back!"

"You can't bring your parents back because you won't help me," Bella said. "If you change your minds and go on the hunt for the five masks . . ."

I started to breathe again. "If we go on the hunt . . ."

"If you recapture all five masks," Bella said, "Screem will lose their evil magic for another year."

"And our house will come back? And our parents?" Peter demanded.

"It's the only way," she said. She brushed her straight black hair back over her shoulder. Her red fingernails glowed in the firelight.

"Here. This will help." She disappeared into the library.

Peter and I gazed at each other but didn't speak. I could tell he was thinking the same thing I was.

The hunt for the masks was crazy. But we had to do it. We had to defeat Screem and get our parents back! Screem's evil magic was real. It wasn't some kind of Halloween joke.

If we wanted to get our lives back to normal, we had to go after him. We had to collect the masks and keep them from him till Halloween was over.

Bella came back into the room. Her long dress trailed behind her. She held a narrow sheet of paper in one hand.

"Here." She pushed it into my hand. "This is a list for you. A list of the five masks."

I raised the paper and read the list out loud: "*Ugly insect; mummy; Himalayan snow wolf; human skull; alien pig creature.*"

"But where do we find them?" Peter asked. "Where do we start?"

"Yes, this is crazy!" I said. "Screem could hide the masks *anywhere*. Where do we begin? We don't have a clue where to search."

She narrowed her eyes at me. "You'll find them, Monica. In fact, sometimes they will find you. *Keeping* them will be harder than finding them. Screem is very tricky. Will you be able to bring them back to me? That's the question."

I didn't really understand what she meant. But I was too jumpy to stand there and talk about it anymore. I wanted to get moving.

Mainly, I wanted to get this night over. I knew there were horrors ahead. But maybe . . . maybe Peter and I could find the five masks and bring back Mom and Dad.

I glanced down. Without realizing it, I had my fingers crossed on both hands.

I didn't have any pockets. So I handed the list of masks to Peter. He tucked it into his pocket.

"Let's go," I said. I started for the door. He followed close behind.

"Wait." Bella hurried after us. "Final instructions."

We turned at the front door.

"You have until dawn," she said. "You must bring the five masks back here, back to me. If you grab one, Screem will try his best to take it away from you."

"How — how can we stop him?" I stuttered.

"Wear the masks you capture," Bella answered. "If you wear a mask, he cannot take it away. Slide one over another. When you are wearing them all, Screem will be powerless."

Powerless.

Was she telling the truth? I hoped so.

I grabbed the doorknob and pulled open the front door. A blast of cold wind pushed against Peter and me.

I ducked my head against the wind and stepped outside.

But Bella's shout made me stop. "Oh, yes," she called. "One thing I forgot to tell you . . ."

12

Bella stepped into the doorway. The wind made her long dress swirl around her. She appeared to fade in the gray light.

"Remember this warning," she said. "Screem has many powers. But his most impressive power is his ability to lie."

The swirling wind made it hard to hear her. "Did you say *lie*?" I shouted.

She nodded. "Screem is the best liar on earth. He's so good, it's almost impossible *not* to believe him."

She pointed her finger at us. "Do not forget this," she said. "Whatever you do, do not believe what he tells you. Do not fall for his lies."

The door closed with a hard thud. Peter and I stood in the sudden darkness. I felt as if I'd been swallowed by the night.

I gasped as the blowing winds suddenly stopped. The silence startled me. Here we were, my brother and I. Alone on this dark, cold Halloween night.

Really alone. More alone than we'd ever been.

And about to do battle with a powerful, evil, lying wizard.

Peter pulled the list of masks from his pocket. It trembled in his hand.

"Where do we go?" he asked, staring into the darkness. "Where do we start?"

I shook my head. I didn't have a clue. I couldn't even begin to think straight.

Peter and I began to jog down the long driveway. At the street, the hedges rose up like dark ocean waves frozen in place.

A tall streetlamp cast a triangle of dim light over the hedges.

"Peter — look." I grabbed his shoulder and stopped him. I pointed to the bottom of the hedge. "See that?"

He squinted hard. "Yes," he answered in a whisper. "Something is tucked in the hedge."

My heart started to pound. "Is it a mask? Is it possible?"

We carefully made our way down the driveway to the hedge.

I dropped to my knees and lowered my head nearly to the ground. Yes. It was a mask.

"The insect mask," Peter whispered.

In the light from above, it looked olive green. It was shaped like a long face, kind of like a grasshopper's. I saw wiry antennae on top of the smooth green head. Tiny black eyes. The mouth hung open, revealing a stringy black forked tongue.

"Wow, that's ugly," Peter said.

I reached out with a trembling hand and touched it. I ran my hand along the top of the head. "I think it's rubber," I whispered. "But . . . it feels . . . *warm*."

"Screem tried to hide it in the hedge," Peter said. "But he didn't hide all of them. This hunt isn't so tough."

I stared at it. Just the sight of the ugly mask sent chill after chill down my back.

"Go ahead. Pick it up," Peter said.

I reached down again — then stopped. "Peter," I whispered, "did he deliberately leave it showing? Is it a *trap*?"

Peter gazed up and down the street. "I don't see anyone, Monica. Grab the mask. Quick. Put it on before Screem comes back for it."

I bent down and reached for the mask. The insect's buggy little eyes gazed up at me. The antennae quivered in a gust of wind.

I picked it up in two hands. I started to pull the mask to my face.

But I stopped with a sharp cry.

"Peter — it . . . it *moved*!" I gasped. "I felt it move! It's . . . ALIVE!"

13

"No way!" Peter exclaimed.

I stretched out the opening and gazed inside the mask.

"Oh, gross!" I cried. "Oh, *sick*!"

I dropped the mask to the grass.

"What *is* it? What's wrong?" Peter asked.

"The mask . . . it's filled with bugs!" I choked out.

"Huh?" He took the mask in his hands and gazed inside the opening. "Oh, wow. It's totally *infested*!"

The mask was *crawling* with fat insects. They scrabbled all over the smooth inside of the mask. They rolled and climbed over each other.

Peter handed the mask back to me. "Monica, you have to put it on," he said. "Before Screem comes back for it."

"But — but —" I sputtered again. "I *can't*, Peter. All those disgusting bugs. There are *hundreds* of them. How can I put it over my face?"

"You *have* to!" Peter cried. "You have to do it, Monica. You heard what Bella said. You have to wear the masks so Screem won't take them back."

I gazed into the mask and felt sick. The bugs were fat and brown and slimy wet.

"We'll take turns," Peter said. "I'll put on the *next* one."

He pushed the mask to my face. "Go ahead. We want to see Mom and Dad again — don't we?"

I stood frozen there, the mask in my hands. A bug crawled out of the mask and walked over my hand. My skin prickled. I wanted to scream.

My stomach was doing flip-flops. I shook the bug off my hand. It was sticky. I could still feel it on my skin.

"Do it, Monica," Peter urged. "Go ahead. Put it on."

I couldn't. No way.

"Do it, Monica," Peter repeated. "Hurry."

My stomach heaved. My throat tightened. I felt like I was about to puke.

I took a deep breath. I shut my eyes.

And I *jammed* the mask down over my head.

I didn't move.

I didn't open my eyes.

The mask fell loosely over my face. I could feel the tiny insect legs poking at my cheeks.

The bugs scrabbled down my cheeks . . . down my neck.

I could feel them on my chin. Feel them trying to squeeze into my mouth.

I couldn't stand it.

I wanted to jump out of my skin.

"Peter — help me!" I shrieked. "They're BITING me! Ohhh . . . help. They're BITING my face!"

14

The pain ended suddenly.

I stopped screaming. A hush fell over me. The only sounds I heard were the pounding of my heart and my wheezing, panting breath.

I opened my eyes. The night was a blur of purple and black.

"Peter?" My voice was muffled by the heavy rubber mask. But at least the bugs were gone. Vanished. "Peter?"

I squinted out through the eyeholes of the insect mask. "Peter!"

Where were we? We weren't standing in front of the tall hedge. We appeared to be in a thick woods.

My eyes finally focused on Peter. To my surprise, he didn't turn to me. He was staring wide-eyed, straight ahead.

I turned to follow his gaze — and cried out in shock.

"Peter — what *are* those things?"

"Big insects," he answered. His whole body shook, but he didn't move his eyes. "They're . . . like giant praying mantises, Monica. A dozen of them. I — I don't believe it!"

"They're taller than we are!" I cried.

The smooth green insects were at least eight feet tall. They had long, slender heads with bulging black eyes as big as teacups on each side. Their antennae swayed in the wind, making a *scup scup scup* sound as they bumped each other.

They stood erect on their back legs. I saw giant wings draped behind their backs like silvery capes.

Their mouths moved up and down rapidly. It took me a while to realize they were chewing. Chewing . . . chewing . . . Their teeth made a grinding sound that made my ears ache.

"It — it's like a *horror* movie," Peter murmured, moving closer to me. "How did this happen?"

"The mask," I said in a whisper. "It must be the evil magic of the mask."

We watched them, listening to their grinding teeth as they kept chewing . . . chewing . . .

And suddenly they were moving forward. Coming at us quickly, antennae whipping the air as they stepped over the tall grass on their broomstick legs.

Grinding . . . grinding . . . grinding . . .

Their huge black eyes glowed as they lowered their flat heads.

"Peter — run!" I gave him a shove and lurched to the side.

"Oh, noooo." I let out a moan. Nowhere to run. The big insects surrounded us. They formed a tight circle, trapping us.

They raised wiry front legs. They rubbed them together in front of their flat chests as they stepped closer.

"Wh-what are they going to do?" Peter stammered. "*Eat* us?"

"The mask," I muttered. "The insect mask is doing this."

I knew what I had to do. I had to pull the evil mask off.

I grabbed the sides and tugged.

No.

It didn't budge.

I grabbed it by the top. But the rubber was too slippery. I couldn't grasp it tightly enough.

Chewing . . . grinding . . . the insects stepped closer. Their antennae waved rapidly over their heads.

Frantic, I grabbed the bottom of the mask. I tried to pull it apart so I could free myself from it.

No. No way.

"Peter — *help* me!" I cried.

Too late.

A giant mantis lowered itself — and bumped its head against the side of my head.

"Owww!" I cried out as pain rocketed down my head, down my body. It felt as if I'd been slammed by a wooden board.

It battered me again. Slammed its long, heavy head into mine.

Stunned, I felt my knees fold. Pain shot through my head and down my whole body.

And before I could move, it lifted me. Lifted me in its short, sticky front legs.

Lifted me off the ground. And pulled me up . . . up . . . toward its enormous grinding teeth.

15

"No! No! NO!"

The screams tore from my throat until I couldn't yell anymore.

I could see gobs of yellow drool on the insect's pointed teeth. The jaw moved back and forth above my head.

It pulled me closer to its grinding teeth. Its head loomed like a gigantic parade balloon.

I thrashed my hands. I kicked my feet.

But the slender front legs gripped me tightly. And raised me higher.

"NOOOOOOO!" Another scream ripped from my mouth and made my throat ache.

The mantis's jaws opened wide.

I tried to squirm. I tried to kick the front of its trunk.

But it held me helpless. And then . . .

To my surprise, it didn't shove me into its grinding mouth. Instead, it turned. And carried me away from the circle of giant insects.

I saw Peter being carried by another insect. The big bug had my brother cradled under one bent leg, pressed against its smooth body.

Peter screamed in protest. But the insect gripped him tightly. He couldn't move.

The two insects carried us side by side. They walked stiffly, their bodies bobbing on their thin legs.

They both stopped suddenly. I glanced down. I saw a line of leafy shrubs.

The insect holding me leaned forward and began to lower me onto a shrub.

I let out a sigh of relief. Did this mean it wasn't going to *eat* me?

The spindly legs lowered me onto my back. I gazed down. The bush was only a few feet tall. Maybe I could drop to my feet and run.

I took a deep breath. I started to move. Slowly, I lowered myself . . .

"YOWWWWW!"

I wailed in pain as the insect jabbed its pointed pincer into my chest. It leaned over me, bringing its head down close to my face. It chomped its jaws.

It kept me pinned down with the sharp pincer pressed against the front of my gymnastics T-shirt. I was trapped on top of the bush. I couldn't move.

"Peter — are you okay?" I called. "Peter?"

I heard him shout from somewhere nearby. I

struggled to turn. But the big mantis had me pinned too tightly to the bush.

I gazed down toward my feet and saw something that filled me with horror.

"No! Oh, please — NO!" I screamed.

The insect was using its other pincer to pull thread from its belly.

Working quickly, it pulled a long line of sticky white thread from its body. And to my horror, it was wrapping the thread around my legs.

Like a spider's webbing. The thread slid out silently, an endless line of it.

The insect worked feverishly, wrapping my knees together tightly now.

"Peter?" I called.

Again, Peter uttered a cry. But he was too far away. I couldn't hear what he was saying.

The insect worked faster. Circling my waist now. Pulling more sticky white string from its belly. Tightening it.

I tried to kick and break through the string, but it was too strong.

The insect held me in place with its sharp pincer and kept spinning the thread, tighter and tighter.

The giant mantis was wrapping me inside a thick cocoon.

"No! Please!" My cries came out shrill and hoarse.

I swung my arms, but I couldn't reach the big insect. I tried to twist my body. Twist myself free.

But the ugly bug had me pinned down. And now it was wrapping its thread around my neck. Round and around.

Working so fast. Spinning. Wrapping me like a caterpillar in a cocoon.

The thread whipped around my neck. And now the insect was starting on the mask that covered my face. It was going to wrap the mask tight to my face in the thick webbing.

The thread swung tightly around the bottom of the mask. In a few seconds, my mouth would be covered.

One last scream.

"Peter!" I cried. "Peter — are you here? DO something!"

16

I heard Peter scream my name. Then his face appeared above mine.

His eyes were wide with fear. His mouth hung open. He was breathing hard.

"I — I broke free," he stammered.

"Do something," I pleaded. "Hurry. I won't be able to breathe inside this cocoon."

Several giant insects lumbered up behind him.

The giant mantis ignored Peter and continued to pull the white webbing around me.

Suddenly, Peter swung away from me. At first, I thought he planned to fight the insects with karate chops and kicks.

But no. He ducked between two big mantises. I saw him dive to the ground.

A second later, he stood up. He raised one hand high. "Monica — look!"

He swung his trick-or-treat bag in the air.

"Hey, look!" he shouted to the huge insects. "Check this out!"

He raised the shopping bag high over his head. Then he dumped all the candy onto the ground.

"Go get it!" Peter cried. He motioned to the candy. "Candy! *Mmmm* good! It's for *you*! Go get it! *Yummm!*"

The insects stood stiffly in a line. Their shiny black eyes appeared to spin. Their mouths moved up and down.

Suddenly, their wings fluttered behind their backs. And they made a high-pitched *eeh eeh eeh* sound. All of them at once. It sounded like a saw cutting through wood.

Their papery wings rose on their backs as they bent their long bodies. They dove for the candy. They grabbed the candy in their jaws.

The *eeh eeh eeh* sound was drowned out by the chomping and grinding as they devoured Peter's trick-or-treat candy.

The big mantis holding me prisoner suddenly froze. The white thread fell slack as the insect stopped spinning its cocoon.

It turned away from me and dove to the ground. Its wings fluttered behind it as it snatched a candy bar in its jaws.

"Peter — hurry," I choked out.

He ducked around the insects and stumbled up to me. He grabbed at the tightly wrapped cocoon and began to tear at it with both hands.

"Hurry," I whispered.

"I — I'm doing my best!" he cried. "It's so sticky and disgusting."

He ripped a section of cocoon off my waist. Then he frantically pulled at the webbing covering my legs.

As he ripped and tore and raked at the thick threads, he kept glancing back at the big insects.

Wings fluttered. The night air rang out with the clatter of grinding teeth.

Peter ripped a section of webbing off my legs. He tried to toss it to the ground. But it stuck wetly to his hand.

I kicked my leg free. I swung around and kicked the other leg out of the cocoon.

My legs tingled and felt numb. I kicked them in the air a few more times, trying to get the blood flowing.

Peter grabbed at the webbing over my hands.

"No," I said. "No time."

I twisted my body and slid down the side of the shrub to the ground. "Let's go," I whispered. "Run!"

Peter took off, running along the row of shrubs, away from the insects.

I stumbled after him. My legs were both still asleep. I couldn't really feel them. And my hands were tied tightly in front of me.

I couldn't get my balance. But I knew we had to run.

The candy wouldn't last forever. And then . . .

"Oh, nooo!" Peter cried, gazing back. "They *see* us! They're coming!"

17

Peter and I turned and ran along a line of tall bushes. I kept losing my balance and stumbling over the leafy ground.

I heard the thud of footsteps. Glancing back, I could see the tall insects leaping after us on their hind legs. Their wings were spread high above their backs. Their antennae fluttered and swayed wildly.

Eeh eeh eeh!

The shrill sound became their battle cry.

They were too tall. Too fast. *No way* could Peter and I outrun them.

"They — they're going to catch us," I choked out, running close behind my brother. "They're going to wrap us both in cocoons."

"No!" Peter shouted. He turned without warning and threw himself into a bush.

In seconds, he disappeared. Pushed his way to the other side.

I glanced back. The giant insects came running toward me. They reached out their spindly front legs, ready to grab me.

I knew I had only seconds to act.

I turned to the bush. So thick. I couldn't find an opening.

The thread over my hands was unraveling. I tugged at it. It was amazingly strong.

I had a crazy idea. Frantically, I pulled off a length of the thread. With a desperate heave, I tossed one end to the top of the bush.

I got lucky. It caught.

As the insects closed in, I took a running leap at the bush. And gripping the thread in both hands, I swung myself out of their grasp. I landed on the top of the bush — and dropped to the other side beside my brother.

Peter jumped back, startled.

We both stood there, hiding behind the solid row of bushes. Inside the insect mask, my face was drenched in sweat. My whole body tingled. Patches of sticky webbing clung to my arms and chest.

Would the ugly mantises come leaping through the bushes?

If they did, they would capture us. Peter and I were too winded to run anymore.

I listened hard. Listened for their tapping footsteps, their *eeh eeh eeh* chirp.

But no. Silence.

I stared through the eyeholes of the mask. I felt cold all over. Pure, cold dread.

But still . . . silence.

I turned — and gasped. I blinked several times, trying to focus my eyes.

Then I grabbed Peter by the shoulder and spun him around. "Look," I said. "Peter — where *are* we? The trees are gone. We're not in the woods. Where has everything gone?"

"It — it's so dark," Peter murmured. "So totally dark."

We were standing nowhere.

I mean, there were no trees. No houses. No moon in the sky.

No sky.

I couldn't see the ground we were standing on.

I spun around. The long row of bushes was gone. Just the inky darkness everywhere.

My ears rang from the silence. A deep hush all around.

"Peter," I whispered, "I don't . . . like . . . this."

18

My body shook. Inside the mask, my teeth began to chatter.

And then the blackness was dotted with grays. I saw mysterious shapes float in front of me. The wind returned, and I heard the crackling swirl of dead autumn leaves.

I heard the rumble of a car. And a low *hoot hoot*. An owl?

Yes. Trees formed out of the darkness. A street. A street I recognized.

A tall, smooth hedge with a house behind it. And I knew the house.

Bella's house.

"We're back," I said. I let out a long sigh of relief.

Peter danced up and down. "We're back! We're back!" He slapped my shoulder. "That was *fun*!"

"Huh?" I jumped away from him. "Are you *crazy*? Do you want to be a caterpillar inside a cocoon? Or eaten by a giant praying mantis?"

"But we're okay!" he cried. "We made it!"

"We're not finished," I reminded him. "We have four more masks to go — remember? And if we don't get them by dawn, we may never see Mom and Dad again."

That took the smile off his face. "Okay. What's the next mask?" he asked.

I turned to Bella's house. The curtains were drawn in the front window. The front light was out. The house was dark.

"I don't believe it," I said. "Did she leave?"

"Forget about her. Let's look for the mummy mask," Peter said. "Bet I know where it is."

He turned and started trotting along the sidewalk. I hurried after him. "Peter, where are you going?"

"The History Museum," he said. "My class had a field trip there last week. They've got a bunch of mummies on display."

I leaned into the gusting wind. "What makes you think the mask will be there?"

"The insect mask was down on the ground with the insects," Peter replied. "I think the masks will tell us where they are hidden. Can you think of a better place for a mummy mask?"

Maybe he was right. We'd soon find out.

The History Museum stood next to the Public Library four or five blocks from our school. They were on a wide street with tall old trees leaning over both sides.

A small grassy park, called Museum Park, stretched across from the museum. Peter and I followed a pool of moonlight across the grass to the museum.

It was a big old-fashioned-looking white stone building with a hundred concrete steps leading up to the entrance. Tall pillars stood on either side of the double doorway. The roof had a white dome over the top.

Lights were on in the museum, but I didn't see anyone around. Two cars came down the street and turned onto Museum Drive.

"No way can we get in through the front," I said. "The doors will be locked tight. And they probably have guards there."

"Last week, my class went in through the back," Peter said. "There are a lot of little doors and windows back there. Maybe we can find a place to sneak in."

We made our way around the side wall. I saw lights on in the tall windows above our heads. But I couldn't see inside.

A black door in a narrow alcove had a sign that read: SERVICE ENTRANCE. The door was locked and chained.

We kept walking. Keeping in the deep shadow of the building, we passed a row of windows with bars over them. Two more doors had chains and padlocks.

I shivered. "This isn't looking good, Peter," I murmured. "What makes you think the mummy mask is in here anyway?"

Before he could answer, I heard a sound. The crackle of dry leaves. Then the scrape and thud of footsteps.

Startled, I jumped. Then I spun around — and gasped.

We were surrounded by mummies. A dozen ragged, decayed mummies.

They came staggering toward us, lumbering silently, arms raised stiffly in front of them.

Backing against the museum wall, I opened my mouth in a shrill scream.

19

One of the mummies laughed. Then several more started to giggle.

Two of them raised their covered hands and bumped knuckles.

"They're . . . kids!" Peter exclaimed. He stood beside me with his back pressed against the cold stone of the museum wall.

Yes. Kids in mummy costumes. Now they were staggering and dancing and skipping toward Museum Drive.

Car doors opened. Parents stepped out to greet them.

A tall woman with a red scarf wrapped around her hair came running up to Peter and me. Her jacket flapped behind her as she ran.

"Is MummyFest over?" she asked breathlessly. "Have they let all the kids out?"

I remembered MummyFest. It was the museum's annual Halloween party. A hundred kids all wrapped up in mummy costumes.

"I think they're letting the kids out now," I said. I turned and saw another group of mummies come dancing out a back door.

The woman let out a relieved sigh. "I thought I was late."

Peter and I followed her to the door. Two kids came running up to her. One of them left a trail of bandages behind her and complained about her bad wrapping job.

When the door opened again to let out more kids, I pulled Peter inside.

I blinked several times as my eyes adjusted to the bright light. We were standing in a big chamber with black and orange streamers stretched across the ceiling.

On a tall pedestal, an enormous jack-o'-lantern glowed with orange and yellow flames inside. Two six-foot-tall mummy statues stood guarding the jack-o'-lantern.

Peter and I gazed around. The room was emptying out fast.

"Which way is the Ancient Egypt section?" I asked.

Peter scrunched up his face. "I think it's back that way." He pointed.

"Let's go," I said.

But before we could move, a man in a stained yellow mummy costume stepped in front of us. His blue eyes stared out at us from inside the mummy head.

He had a tall black top hat tilting on top of his head. A round button on the hat read: TAKE ME TO MY MUMMY.

"Can I help you?" he asked. "Are you picking up someone?"

I nodded. "Yes. Our little sister. Franny. Have you seen her? Has she come out?"

He squinted at me. Did he believe me?

"There are still some kids in the cafeteria," he said. "Why don't you try there?" He pointed to an open archway against the back wall.

"Hey, thanks," I said. I gave Peter's arm a tug, and we began to jog toward the archway.

"I *love* your bug mask," the man shouted after me.

I shouted thanks but didn't turn back.

Peter and I trotted straight ahead. I called, "Franny! Franny!" until we were out of the man's sight.

"That was easier than I thought," Peter said.

"We're not there yet," I told him.

We hurried down a long, brightly lit hall. Up ahead, I could hear kids' voices and people laughing.

We passed glass cases in the wall displaying blue and orange vases. Some of the vases were cracked and chipped. They looked very old.

The cafeteria came into view. I saw only a few kids in there. They were sitting on the floor, talking and eating candy bars.

Some white-uniformed workers had started to clean up. They were sweeping the floor and picking up candy wrappers and other trash.

Peter and I didn't stop at the cafeteria. We turned a corner and kept going.

An arrow sign read: EGYPTIAN GALLERIES.

"The mummy rooms are right up there," Peter said.

We started to jog faster. The lights in this hallway were dimmer. Long shadows swept over the floor.

I could see the entrance to the Egyptian Galleries up ahead.

We were only a few feet away — when a deep, angry voice boomed out: *"Stop right there! Where do you think you're going?"*

20

Caught.

I spun around. I saw a dark-uniformed guard trotting toward us.

I started to say something.

But he turned. Two kids in mummy costumes stepped out from an alcove.

"Where do you think you're going?" the guard repeated.

"We couldn't find the front door," one of the kids told him.

He took the kid's hand. "Follow me. You're going the wrong way." He led them back toward the cafeteria.

Peter and I were pressed against the wall. I realized I was holding my breath. I let it out in a long stream.

"I — I thought he caught us," I said.

"Me, too," Peter muttered. "That was close."

We turned and ducked into the door marked

EGYPTIAN GALLERIES. The lights in the big room were dimmed. The air felt hot and damp.

We stayed against the wall. I gazed all around, searching for any guards. The room was empty.

I counted four mummy cases, one in each corner of the room. A model of a pyramid stood in the center. One wall was covered with photos of the pyramids. Display cases on the other walls showed jewelry and other objects from ancient Egypt.

Peter and I circled the room. My eyes squinted in the dim light.

I examined the display cases. I walked around the model pyramid and all around each mummy case.

"I don't see a mummy mask," I whispered. "Maybe Screem didn't hide it here. Maybe we should leave before we're caught."

I started for the door, but Peter stepped in front of me.

"The mummy cases," he said. "We have to look inside them."

"But —" I started to protest. The ancient cases were of carved heavy stone. The lids would be impossible to lift.

"Screem hid the mask inside one of them," Peter said. "I know it. I just know it."

I groaned. Peter is so stubborn. "But how do we look inside? How can we lift the heavy lids?"

I heard a noise outside the room. I ducked behind a mummy case.

Footsteps. Peering around the side, I saw two guards walk past the gallery.

My heart thudded in my chest. Breaking into the museum had to be a serious crime. If we were caught . . .

If we were caught, no one would believe we were searching the mummy cases for a mummy mask. We would be in major trouble.

But we were already in major trouble, I decided.

What could be bigger trouble than having your house and parents disappear?

I stood up and turned to the mummy case. I moved to the center of the case and grabbed the lid with both hands.

The lid felt surprisingly cool. It had a pharaoh's head carved at one end. The eyes were blank. Part of the pharaoh's headdress was broken off.

I started to push up on the lid, but I hesitated.

A lot of people are really into mummies. The four mummies are the most popular things in the museum.

I'm not a big mummy person. I mean, they *are* dead people, after all. Dead people who have been rotting and decaying inside tar and bandages for a few thousand years.

Okay, Monica, you can do this, I told myself.

I gripped the edge of the heavy stone lid, braced myself, steadied my legs —

— and pushed the lid up with a groan.

To my surprise, it slid up easily.

The lid swung out of my hand and started to slide off the other side of the case.

"Nooo!" I let out a cry. I couldn't let it crash to the floor.

I jumped and made a wild grab for it with both hands.

Missed.

And went sailing headfirst, down into the mummy case.

21

"*Ooof.*" I landed flat on my stomach on top of the mummy. I bounced once — and my face sank into the hard, smelly wrappings of the mummy's chest.

I raised my head and let out a groan.

The mummy wrappings were dry and scratchy. My cheeks itched.

I gagged as the putrid stench from the ancient corpse rose to my nostrils. I struggled to keep my dinner down. Wave after wave of the sour odor swept over me.

I was sprawled flat on top of the mummy. It felt hard as bones beneath me. It was tiny, like a child. Its wrapped head was no bigger than a lightbulb.

The ancient gauze over the mummy's head dipped where the eyes had been. Dried tar stained the wrappings around the neck.

The odor sickened me. I tried to close my nose and breathe out of my mouth.

Carefully, I struggled onto my side. The mummy moved beneath me.

Gross.

I gazed up. The lid had slid only halfway off the top of the case. Dim light poured over me from the ceiling.

I worked myself to a sitting position. Then I grabbed the edge of the lid. My idea was to hold on to the lid and pull myself out.

But as I tugged, I heard a grinding sound. Stone against stone.

It took me only a second to realize the heavy lid was falling . . . falling into the mummy case.

I'm going to be CRUSHED.

I swung away from the falling lid. Grabbed the side of the case with both hands. And flipped myself out.

I fell free of the case — just as the lid crashed down inside it.

The roar rocked the room.

I rolled away from the case. Stopped in front of the pyramid model.

Then I lay there on the floor for a long moment, catching my breath.

The sour, putrid odor of the mummy lingered on my clothes. It clung to the inside of the insect mask.

I grabbed at the mask. I wanted to pull it off. I wanted Halloween to be over. To be out of this museum where we didn't belong. To be home safe in my house with my parents.

My parents.

That thought made me remember why I couldn't remove the mask.

I stood up and brushed the thick dust off the front of my clothing. Then I gazed around the room.

"Peter?" I called.

My eyes swept the room, from mummy case to mummy case.

"Peter? Where are you?"

No answer.

I had a heavy feeling in the pit of my stomach.

"Peter? Come on. You're not funny. We have to get out of here. Peter? Where are you?"

My voice grew higher and more shrill with every word.

"Peter? Please?" I cried. "Peter?"

He had disappeared.

22

I couldn't move. Couldn't breathe.

I heard voices outside the gallery.

I ducked behind the pyramid and listened. I peered around the side and saw the same two dark-uniformed guards walk past the doorway. They were shaking their heads and laughing about something.

"Peter?" I called out in a tiny voice.

A second later, I heard his cry. "Got it!"

I let out a shout when his head popped up from one of the mummy cases. He raised a hand high. He waved the mummy mask in the air.

"Help me." He stuck his hand out the side. I grabbed it and helped tug him to the floor.

He raised the mask in one hand. I squeezed it. It felt like rubber. The eyes were sunken. The wrappings around it appeared torn and stained.

"I knew it would be in here," Peter said. He pumped his other fist in the air.

"You scared me to death," I said.

"At least I found the —"

He stopped. We both heard voices. And footsteps outside the door.

The two security guards had just passed. Who was coming?

Was it Screem?

"Quick, Peter —" I shoved the mask toward his face. "Your turn. Put it on."

He held the mask in two hands and raised it to his head. Then he hesitated.

The footsteps grew louder. Closer.

"Peter — quick!" I whispered.

"I . . . can't," he said. He twisted his face in disgust. "The mask . . . it's filled with dust. Mummy dust. It — it smells like something dead."

"I don't care," I said. I pushed it toward his face again. "Put it on. Hurry, Peter!"

"Ohhh." He let out a groan. He stared into the mask. "It's . . . *sick*," he murmured.

Then he raised the mask above his head.

Just as the two security guards burst into the room.

23

Their eyes bulged and their mouths opened in alarm when they saw us.

"Hold it! Stop right there! Don't move!" one of them shouted angrily.

"How did you kids get back here?" his partner cried.

They moved toward us quickly, hands out at their sides as if they expected a fight.

"Uh . . . we were at the mummy party," I stammered. "We . . . couldn't find the exit, and —"

Their boots thudded on the marble floor as they strode toward us.

"You'd better tell the truth," one of them said. "You two are in a world of trouble."

"Trespassing on city property is a serious crime," his partner said.

I turned to my brother. His face was tight with fear. And then he let out a cry — and jammed the mummy mask down over his head.

A blinding flash of white light made me scream.

I shut my eyes tight, but the light didn't fade. It grew brighter . . . brighter . . . until I felt my head was about to explode.

Then . . . solid darkness. Blacker than black.

Slowly, I opened my eyes. The museum room had vanished. I stared up at a cloudy sky.

It took me a long moment to realize I was stretched out on my back. I was lying on something flat and hard. Above me, the sky darkened. The clouds seemed to be coming closer and closer as if they were going to smother me.

"Peter?" My voice came out in a choked whisper.

I turned to see him close beside me. The mummy mask covered his face.

He was also on his back. I could see he was lying on some kind of wooden stretcher. "Where are we?" he murmured. "The mask . . ."

"The mask must have taken us here," I said. "Every time we put on a mask, it — it —"

My words caught in my throat. I realized my hands were strapped down. I couldn't get up from the wooden stretcher.

I couldn't jump down.

I gazed straight ahead. Peter and I were lying between two rows of white-robed men. The two long lines of men seemed to stretch for miles.

The men were all shaved bald. Their dark heads glowed in the eerie light seeping through the clouds.

They were humming. Humming the same low note endlessly. It sounded more like a roar than music. They kept raising and bowing their heads as they hummed.

I squinted into the distance, where an orange stone building rose toward the sky. A giant sculpture of a cat stood beside the building. I could see a blue-green platform with tall flames rising behind it.

It's an altar, I thought. *They had one in a mummy movie Peter and I watched once.*

I gazed down from the stretcher. We were on sand. I turned — and saw a familiar shape on the horizon. A pyramid?

"Peter, I think the mummy mask took us to Egypt," I said. "Ancient Egypt."

He tried to sit up. But his hands were strapped down, too. "I don't like this, Monica. Why are these bald dudes humming like that?"

"I think they're praying," I said.

"We have to get out of here," Peter said.

Well, duh.

Several white-robed bald men surrounded us. They all had deep, dark eyes. Their eyebrows had been shaved off.

Six men grabbed the sides of my stretcher and lifted it off the sand. Their arm muscles rippled.

They didn't look at us. They stared straight ahead at the huge cat sculpture.

The drone of voices grew louder. It sounded like a million buzzing bees.

The men hoisted our stretchers onto their shoulders and began carrying us between the endless lines of white-robed Egyptians.

"Let us down!" I cried. "Can you understand me? Let us down!" I tugged at the straps over my wrists.

They moved slowly, steadily, eyes straight ahead.

"Let us down!" I screamed again.

The sky grew even darker. I squinted through the dim light to the fiery altar in front of the wall. Two men in tall white hats stood together, waiting for us. Their robes were bright blue. They had huge red jewels hanging around their necks.

"Priests," I muttered.

The hum of the deep note rang in my ears. I wanted to cover my ears. To shut out the frightening sound.

Face after face swept by.

Their eyes followed Peter and me as we bounced past them, strapped to the wooden stretchers.

I smelled something strong. I took a deep breath. Another. A sharp odor filled my nose.

It took me a few seconds to recognize it.

Tar.

The drone of the deep voices made me want to scream. The faces rolled past, so solemn, the eyes so blank.

The two blue-robed priests stepped forward as Peter and I came near. Their cone-shaped hats pointed straight up to the sky.

The tar smell brought tears to my eyes.

I turned and spotted something at the side of the altar.

It was an enormous round cauldron. Like one of those big cooking pots that witches always have, only five times as big.

Inside it, I could see the tar bubbling. Yes. Steaming hot tar.

Peter and I were being carried to a cauldron of boiling tar.

"Oh, nooooo." A moan escaped my throat. My whole body shuddered in terror.

Because suddenly, every horror movie . . . every mummy movie I'd ever seen . . . came back to me. And I knew why we were being carried through this ancient Egyptian temple.

We were about to be mummified . . . mummified *alive*.

24

As we came closer, I could hear the fire crackling behind the altar. I saw piles of cloth at one corner of the platform. Cloth to cover the tar? Cloth to cover our tarred bodies?

My panic made everything a blur. The altar . . . the two waiting priests . . . the jewels around their necks . . . the rows of humming men . . .

The cauldron made a popping sound. I saw a wave of steaming tar roll across its surface.

I turned to Peter. Did he realize what was about to happen?

I couldn't see his face. It was hidden beneath the mummy mask. The evil mummy mask had brought us here. Brought us to this horror.

The humming faded behind us. The crackle of the fire grew louder.

We moved into the shadow of the tall cat sculpture. Up close, the cat looked like a wild creature. More like a tiger than a cat.

The priests stepped forward. Their robes rustled as they walked.

Our stretchers came to a sharp stop. The men released the wrist straps. They began to lower Peter and me to the sand.

I struggled to stop my brain from whirring. I needed to think straight. How could we escape this?

I couldn't think of a thing.

I watched as two men lifted Peter off his stretcher. They set him on his feet. They held his arms and forced him toward the priests.

Peter squirmed and struggled. He tried to twist out of their grasp. But the men were too strong for him.

"Monica! Help me!" Peter wailed. His eyes were on the cauldron of tar. He knew what was about to happen to us.

"Monica! Don't let them!" he screamed. "Don't let them!"

The priests led the way to the cauldron.

A hush fell over the temple. The long lines of worshippers grew silent. So silent I could hear the rush of wind over the desert sands.

The two men held Peter in place.

He kicked one of them hard in the ankle. But the man didn't cry out or move or react in any way.

Peter squirmed and twisted. The men held on tightly.

The priests stepped up to the boiling tar cauldron. Wisps of steam rose up all around. The sharp odor made tears pour down my face.

The priests held the red jewels in front of them and began swinging them from side to side. They began to chant strange words in deep, low tones.

"Let me go!" Peter screamed. "You can't do this! We don't belong here! We're from America!"

The priests swung the red jewels and chanted as if Peter wasn't standing there screaming at them.

Then one of them motioned with both hands toward the cauldron.

The two men lifted Peter off his feet.

He kicked furiously and screamed his head off. But he was helpless against them.

They raised him higher.

I knew I had to do something. I had only seconds.

The men raised Peter high over the cauldron.

Too late, I realized. I let out a long moan of horror.

Too late.

25

The men held Peter over the bubbling cauldron. His kicking feet were just inches above the tar.

He twisted and squirmed. He screamed and begged.

I took a deep shuddering breath.

Maybe . . . Maybe I could do something. . . .

I didn't even plan it. I suddenly sprang forward. I guess after so much gymnastics practice, the moves just came naturally to me.

I flipped onto my hands. Did a handstand on the edge of my stretcher.

Then I did a forward pike roll — up and over the heads of the men holding me captive.

I dropped hard onto the sand. Leaned far over and did another forward pike.

I sailed high — and landed both feet on the nearest priest's chest.

Startled, he made a choking sound. His mouth dropped open as my kick sent him stumbling back.

I landed on my feet and watched as he went toppling into the boiling cauldron.

He splashed onto his back in the hot muck. Tar rolled over the sides of the cauldron.

Shrieking at the top of his lungs, he smacked his arms against the surface of the tar.

Cries of panic and shock rang out over the temple. Everyone moved at once.

The two men holding Peter set him down on the ground. They leaned over the steaming cauldron and grabbed wildly at the robe of the screaming priest.

The other priest dropped to his knees in shock. He shut his eyes and raised his hands to the giant cat sculpture.

White-robed men rushed to help pull the screaming priest from the cauldron.

I grabbed Peter. "Let's go."

26

We took off, running hard.

I led the way toward the front of the temple. Glancing back, I could see the men still struggling over the boiling cauldron.

We ran along the side of the temple to the back. No one followed us.

We stopped and stared into the distance. Nothing but sand. Behind the temple, the desert seemed to stretch on forever.

Peter put his hands on his knees and struggled to catch his breath. "Wow! Was that a close call!" he said. His voice was muffled by the mummy mask.

He raised a foot. "Look. I have tar stuck to the bottom of my shoe."

I shuddered. "I don't want to think about it. What are we going to do now? How are we going to get home?"

The sky darkened. The wind grew colder.

The sand shifted and moved like ocean waves.

A hard gust of wind sent a burst of sand into my eyes. I cried out. It felt sharp, like cut glass.

The wind howled. Sand seemed to rise up from the ground, wave after wave.

Peter and I covered our heads. The sand swept over us. Pounded us. It felt as if my skin was erupting in a thousand cuts.

I struggled to breathe.

Another high wave of sand crashed into me. I toppled into the temple wall.

I couldn't see. All I could hear was the roar of the wind and the crash of the sand.

And then . . . silence.

The sandstorm stopped as suddenly as it had started.

I took one deep breath after another. I brushed sand off my costume with both hands.

Peter turned to me, dazed. He shook his head, and sand flew out of the mask in all directions.

"Scary," he muttered.

I glanced at the temple wall. Whoa. Wait a minute.

Was that door there before?

I stared at the door. And a row of windows next to the door. A sign read: SERVICE ENTRANCE. ALL DELIVERIES HERE.

I stepped away from the wall. “Peter — look!” I cried.

I recognized where we were.

“Peter,” I said. “We’re at the back of the History Museum.”

We heard a horn honk. Two cars rolled along Museum Drive.

We stood there for a long moment, catching our breath.

“We’re back — and we have two masks,” Peter said finally.

I sighed. “It wasn’t exactly easy,” I said. “My eyes still sting from that sandstorm. And I can still smell the boiling tar.”

Peter pulled out the list of masks. “We have to keep going,” he said. “It must be getting late.”

He read the list. “The Himalayan snow wolf mask is next.”

I stared at him. “Himalayan snow wolf? We talked about them in school. They live in the Himalayan Mountains.”

“Is that far?” Peter asked.

I think he was joking.

“The snow wolves live on snowy mountain peaks,” I said. “We don’t have any snowy mountain peaks. We don’t have any mountains in Hillcrest.”

“So . . . where would Screem hide a snow wolf mask?” Peter asked. “A wolf preserve?”

"Our town doesn't have a wolf preserve," I said.

Peter banged his head with both fists. "Think. Think," he urged himself. "Where would Screem hide a snow wolf mask?"

Suddenly, I had an idea.

27

"Are we really going to climb this in the dark?"

Peter didn't sound like his usual crazy, energetic self. He sounded afraid.

I pointed to the sky. "The moon came out," I said. "Look. It's lighting the path for us."

Peter gazed up the hill. "But the path curves around the hill. Some of it will be totally dark. And it's so steep —"

I patted his shoulder. "This is the only steep hill in town. The only hill that's a little like a mountain. And it's even called Wolf Hill!"

"But we don't know the mask is up there," Peter said. "What if we climb all the way to the top and there's no mask?"

"Then we look somewhere else," I said.

His whole body sagged. Like a balloon losing its air.

"Come on, Peter. Step up," I said. "This isn't like you. Normally, you'd be dancing up this hill."

"But . . . this whole thing is impossible," he whined.

"Of course it's impossible," I said. "But we have to do it."

Leaning into the wind, I turned and started up the path. My shoes slid on the gravelly, sandy surface.

I glanced back. Peter was following close behind, kicking small stones out of the way as he climbed.

It's funny that our town is called Hillcrest. Because it's very flat. There are only a few big hills in the whole city.

Wolf Hill is the steepest hill in town. It rises up over our small downtown section. Hillcrest ends at the hill. On the other side, there is only farmland.

You can't drive to the top because there's no road. There's only a rocky dirt path that curves around and around as it takes you up the hill.

Hikers like to climb Wolf Hill because of the amazing view of the town down below. Last winter, some crazy teenagers tried snow-boarding near the top. They nearly sailed off the rocky cliffs. Police got there before anyone was hurt.

The sand gave way to gravel and stone as I pulled myself up the path. The half-moon sent pale light in front of me like a spotlight. But the path kept turning away from the light. I struggled not to stumble in the long dark patches.

"Peter, how you doing?" I called back to him.

He mumbled an answer. He had fallen behind. I stopped to take a breath and let him catch up.

The wind whistled around the hillside. There were no trees up here. Tall weeds jutted up on both sides of the path. They swayed and rustled in the wind.

Just above us, the path led right out onto a narrow rock cliff. Peter stepped past me and peered down the side of the cliff. "Wow. We're up pretty high," he said.

He stepped out onto the rock. Then he raised his hands in the air and screamed, "I'm falling! Help! I'm falling!"

My heart skipped a beat. I dove forward and grabbed his arm.

He laughed. "Gotcha." He backed off the rock. "Just wanted to give you a thrill."

I let out a groan. "Peter, you are *so* not funny." My heart was still pounding.

That dumb joke made me angry. But in a way I was glad to see the old Peter back.

I gave him a push. "Keep climbing. We have to get to the very top."

His eyes peered out at me from beneath the mummy mask. "Do you really think the snow wolf mask is up there?"

I shrugged. "Who knows? I just think if I was Screem, that's where I'd hide it."

I moved past him and, leaning forward, continued to climb. The path curved sharply and grew steeper as we followed it up.

Rocks slid under my shoes and went tumbling over the cliff side. I nearly fell into a shallow rut. I twisted my ankle. Stopped for the pain to fade. Then continued up.

We climbed for another ten minutes or so.

"Peter?" I turned back to see how he was doing.

And felt the ground move.

It took me a second or two to realize my shoes were sliding on loose stones. I lurched back, struggling to catch my balance.

But my feet slid off the path. My legs went out from under me.

And I dropped over the cliff side.

And fell, screaming all the way down.

28

My scream cut off as I hit a rock ledge below. I landed on my stomach.

My hands slapped the stone surface and kept my head from bouncing on the rock. I felt my breath rush out in a whoosh.

I started to choke. Gasping, I struggled to pull air into my lungs.

I crouched on my hands and knees, finally breathing normally. I shut my eyes to stop the world from spinning.

I heard Peter calling to me from the path above. His head peeked over the cliff edge. I waved to him.

"I'm okay!" I shouted.

I gazed around. I hadn't fallen very far. I had landed on a wide rock ledge. Smooth stone, white in the moonlight.

Squinting hard, I could see the path at the far end of the ledge. No problem getting back up to Peter.

I pulled myself to my feet. I took a step away from the cliff edge, toward the path.

Then I stopped. And stared at the face peering at me from the path.

At first I thought it was Peter. I thought he had come down to help me.

Then I saw that it wasn't human. It was an animal.

It didn't move. It kept its head low, as if ready to attack.

I gasped when I realized I was staring at an angry snow wolf.

Whoa. Wait. Not a wolf.

I squinted hard. It took a few seconds to realize what I was seeing. A dark animal wearing the snow wolf mask.

I lurched forward. Stretched out both hands — and grabbed at the mask. The creature uttered a low growl.

The mask snapped off. I snatched it away and stared in surprise at the snarling animal.

A dog.

A giant black dog. Its eyes glowed red. It bared its teeth and snapped at me.

Gripping the mask in both hands, I jumped back.

The dog lowered its head again and growled. Its red eyes glared up at me angrily.

I took another step back.

The dog moved onto the rock ledge. It had me

trapped. It was too big for me to edge past it. And if I took another step or two back, I'd step off the cliff.

"Nice doggy. Nice doggy," I said.

It growled and bared its teeth in reply.

The big dog arched its back. It was getting ready to attack.

I struggled to think. Could I do a forward roll over the dog, onto the safety of solid ground?

Maybe a simple cartwheel?

No time. The big creature roared as it leaped at me.

It lowered its heavy paws onto my shoulders — and sank its teeth into my neck.

29

"Owwwwww."

With a shrill cry of pain, I shrugged my shoulder and shoved the dog off. I raised the snow wolf mask in both hands. I knew it would take me somewhere weird and frightening. But I had no choice. I had to get away from the vicious dog.

I took a deep breath — and jammed the wolf mask down over the insect mask.

And then a blinding flash of light made me shut my eyes.

The light seemed to swirl around me. Cover me like a weightless blanket.

I waited for the jolt of pain of the dog's bite. But I didn't feel it.

I couldn't feel anything. Just the coldness of the white light.

Cold. So cold.

I opened my eyes and gasped. I was standing in deep snow.

A bright moon low overhead made the snow gleam like silver. I blinked, waiting for my eyes to adjust.

I glanced around. The snowy ground dipped, then rose again. A tall, white mountain peak loomed in front of me. And to my side, a snowy cliff with nothing but purple sky behind it.

I'm in the mountains, I realized. *Snowy mountains.*

Where had the mask taken me? I sniffed the air. I smelled something new. I couldn't quite place the smell.

I took a few unsteady steps forward in the snow. The snow was soft and flaky and fell away from me as I walked.

I gazed down at a set of paw prints. Animal paws making a straight track along the side of the cliff.

I stopped after another few steps. I felt awkward. Heavy. As if I'd put on a lot of weight.

A picture flashed into my mind. I saw a rabbit. The rabbit was dead and torn to pieces. I could *smell* the dead, raw rabbit. I could see its meaty legs and its tender middle. The red meat clinging to its bones.

I felt hungry.

Wait. Stop, Monica. Why the crazy thoughts?

My stomach growled. I sniffed the air again. I recognized the smell. A human. I was picking up the scent of a nearby human.

I turned slowly — and saw Peter standing on top of a low snowdrift. His mummy mask gleamed under the moonlight. He had his hands wrapped tightly around himself.

"Peter?"

I tried to call to him. But only a grunt escaped my throat.

I tried again. And grunted again.

What's up with this?

I lowered my gaze to the snow. I stared at the animal paw prints. They stretched in a straight line from *behind* me.

They were *mine*!

My stomach growled again. I felt like growling, too. I suddenly felt an anger I'd never felt before. Pure animal anger.

I'm an animal.

The words rang in my ears. And repeated. *I'm an animal.*

So that's what the wolf mask had done. It carried Peter and me here to this high, snowy mountain slope. And it turned *me* into a snow wolf.

A grunting snow wolf staggering forward on four legs.

Hungry. And angry.

I pawed the snow. I looked around.

I pictured the dead rabbit again. I could taste its cold, wet, pink-and-yellow insides. What tasty morsels did the stomach hold?

I raised my head to the sky and let the wind tickle the fur on my ears. Then I sniffed again. Humans were too bony to eat. But Peter had such a sweet scent.

I started to drool. My belly grumbled.

Peter might steal my rabbit. I pictured him grabbing the rabbit in two hands. Ripping it apart. Tossing the fur into the snow and raising the fresh, tasty meat to his face.

No way.

Peter can't have my food. A wolf doesn't share.

I knew what I had to do. I had to get rid of Peter.

He stood watching me.

And I can smell his fear.

I staggered toward him on my strong animal legs.

He let out a cry and stumbled backward, off the snowdrift.

He landed on his back in the deep snow.

I didn't give him time to stand up.

I pounced.

I clamped my teeth onto his neck and scooped him up in both front paws. Then I raised myself onto my back legs. With my new animal strength, I lifted him above my head.

I released his neck and opened my mouth in a howl of victory. My howl echoed off the high mountains above us.

The long triumphant howl burst from my chest and out through my open snout. It felt good to show off my strength.

Peter screamed and struggled, kicking and thrashing.

But he was no match for my animal power.

When the wolf is angry, the wolf will ACT.

Holding the shrieking boy in my claws, I staggered on my hind legs to the edge of the snowy cliff.

And with a beastly roar, I tossed him over the side.

30

Peter flew into the air.

His scream of horror *snapped* something in my brain — and I lunged forward. Closed my jaw on to the edge of his karate uniform. Caught him between my sharp teeth. Swung him to safety.

I held him down with both paws. And waited for my mind to clear.

My animal thoughts flashed past me in a jumble of pictures and odors. I could smell the blood of the raw rabbit. I pictured my paw prints in the snow.

And suddenly, in my mind I was running through the snow, running on all fours. Kicking up a mist of white behind me.

Then that picture was replaced by another — Peter at home. Our house. Our front yard.

I could smell the fallen brown leaves. Smell the tangy aroma of wood fires burning in fireplaces around our neighborhood.

Peter's screaming rang in my sensitive wolf ears.

The sound brought me back. Brought me back to being me.

I'm Monica.

I spun away from the snow-covered cliff. I set Peter free.

He stood up and stumbled awkwardly. His knees appeared to give way. But he stayed on his feet.

And he continued to scream.

And without realizing it, I was screaming, too.

I raised my head to the sky. Then I opened my jaws and bellowed at the pale moon.

We stood together screaming. I only stopped when I felt the ground tremble beneath my hind paws.

In the sudden hush, I heard a distant rumble.

Thunder?

The rumble grew louder until it became a ground-shaking roar.

Following the sound, I gazed up to the mountains above us. And saw a tidal wave — a high tidal wave of snow cascading down at us.

An avalanche!

Our screams had shaken the snow loose from the mountaintop. We had started an avalanche.

It came tumbling down with a deafening roar. Picking up speed, the wave of white rose higher and higher until the dark sky disappeared behind it.

Enormous boulders of snow came falling in front of the wave. They bounced and tumbled down the mountainside.

The whole world was white.

It fell over us. Battered us. Then buried us.

So cold. So icy cold.

I reached for Peter but couldn't find him.

And I sank deep, deep into the rushing wave of snow.

31

I couldn't breathe. I couldn't move. Except to shiver under the heavy blanket of icy snow.

I struggled to force down my panic. I knew I had to move — *now.*

Using all my strength, I grabbed the snow above me and pulled myself up.

I moved only a few inches. But it gave me space to kick my feet.

Kicking and thrashing, I dug my way to the surface. With a last burst of strength, I pulled myself out of the deep snow. Then I raised my face to the sky and sucked in breath after breath of the cool, fresh air.

"Hey, look." A voice beside me. I turned to see Peter. He had pulled himself up, too.

He pointed to a dark strip of red light in the sky. The color stretched along a black horizon.

Peter's face was hidden by the mummy mask.

He turned to me. "Where are we?" His voice came out muffled and tiny.

I didn't answer right away. I gazed into the strip of red-purple light. "That's . . . the sun starting to come up," I said. "The snow . . . the avalanche . . . it must have taken us away from there. . . . It brought us back."

I spoke in *my* voice. My *human* voice. I was me again. No longer a four-legged animal.

And we were standing on a street, gazing into the night.

Peter followed my gaze. Then a cry escaped his throat. "The snow is gone! Monica, we're *alive*! The snow . . . the mountains — all gone!"

I swallowed. My throat ached from screaming. "Peter," I said, "Look at me. Am I . . . back? Back to normal?"

He squinted at me. "You were *never* normal!" he said. He laughed at his own joke.

I gazed down at myself. It was hard to see. I had two masks on my face, one on top of the other.

But I was me again. Shivering in the autumn cold in my little gymnastics costume.

I glanced around. We were standing on the sidewalk on a block of dark houses. An empty lot across the street.

It took me a few seconds to realize we were standing right where our house used to be.

The sight of the bare lot sent a wave of sadness over me.

I turned to Peter. "We don't have a lot of time left," I said.

Peter nodded. He shoved his hands into the pockets of his white uniform. "I — I can't believe what's happened to us tonight," he said softly.

"I'm afraid to find another mask," I confessed. "Afraid to put another mask on. Each time it — it takes us into a *horror* movie."

"Except it's all real," he said. "But, Monica — we have to keep going. We only have three masks." He stared at the empty lot in front of us.

"We don't have much time," I said.

"How about the skull mask?" he said. "That should be easy to find."

I squinted at him. "Easy? Why?"

He shrugged. "So far, the masks have been their own clues — so . . ."

I finished his sentence. "The best place to find a skull mask is . . . a graveyard."

We both began walking in the same direction. Hillcrest's oldest graveyard was about a three-block walk.

The night was eerily still. The houses we passed were all dark. No cars on the street. The trees didn't rustle. No whisper of wind.

The only sounds were our shoes thudding on the sidewalk and the beating of my heart.

I had to jog to catch up to Peter. "Are we — are we really going into the old graveyard on Halloween?"

"What's scary about it?" Peter demanded. "It's only dead people."

32

The paint had nearly all peeled off the low picket fence in front of the graveyard. Parts of the fence had fallen to the ground, leaving wide gaps.

I peered through one of the gaps at the crooked, tilting gravestones, which were black against the purple sky. Dead leaves had piled up and formed hills against several gravestones. Like blankets to cover the dead.

I shuddered.

I never liked cemeteries. Even new, pretty ones that were well taken care of with smooth grass and straight, shiny gravestones.

Some of my friends sometimes had picnics in the new cemetery a few blocks from school. But I couldn't join them. It gave me the creeps.

I just couldn't stop thinking about the dead people lying so still, rotting away in their wormy coffins beneath the ground.

I had nightmares about graveyards. I never

told anyone about them. I didn't know if it was normal or not.

And now, Peter and I stood staring through the broken fence. Gazing at the crooked rows of little grave markers and the blanket of dead leaves over them.

"Let's go," Peter said. He squeezed through a gap in the fence.

I took a deep breath and followed him.

As soon as we stepped into the graveyard, the wind started up again. It had been so still and silent. And now, it was as if the wind had been waiting for us.

The dead leaves began to crackle and move. Carried on the wind, the fat brown leaves danced in circles around the low grave markers.

The bare limbs of the old trees appeared to shudder in the swirling gusts.

"Peter . . . I d-don't like this," I stammered.

He moved down a row of gravestones. Most of them had fallen over and lay flat on their backs. *Like the dead people beneath them,* I thought.

"Peter?"

He didn't seem to hear me. Leaning into the wind, he moved down the row of ancient gravestones. I followed close behind.

I kept my eyes on the ground. Was the skull mask hidden here? Was it buried in the deep leaves? Hidden behind a grave?

I grabbed Peter's arm when I heard a loud moan.

"What was *that*?" I cried. "Did you hear it?"

He spun back to me. "Hear what?"

"A moan. Like someone groaning," I said. "It . . . sounded human," I insisted.

"Look around," he said. He waved his arm. "We're the only ones here."

"The only *living* ones here," I corrected him.

He wandered down the next row of old graves. His shoes crunched loudly over the dry leaves. The trees creaked all around.

I jumped in shock when a flat gray headstone toppled over at my feet. I leaped back, my heart pounding.

Just the wind.

And then I heard the moan again.

"Peter," I called in a trembling voice. "We . . . we're not alone."

33

We both stopped and listened. Where was that frightening moaning sound coming from?

Like a sad cry from the grave, I told myself.

Then I saw a blur of yellow-white. A pale spot of light.

I took a few steps over the crackling leaves. I moved closer, squinting hard.

"Peter — do you see this?" I pointed.

He turned from the row of graves. He followed my gaze.

I took another few steps closer to it.

I saw a deep hole, black against the gray of the ground. An open grave.

Beside the grave, I saw some narrow tombstones. Unmarked. Tilting this way and that.

And at the head of the open grave . . . a wider grave marker. Like a stone tablet.

With a yellow object resting on top of it.

The mask!

The skull mask. I could see it clearly now. I could see its deep eyeholes. The open jaw slack against the front of the gravestone.

"Peter! Here it is!" I shouted. "I found it."

He cried out. I could hear him running to me.

I stepped up to the mask. I bent down.

The skull had a hideous toothy grin on its sagging mouth. The top of the head was bumpy and crisscrossed with cracks.

I raised both hands. I hesitated for a moment. I knew something weird was about to happen. But I had no choice.

I grabbed the skull mask by the sides.

Oh, no.

Oh, no.

I opened my mouth in a shriek of cold terror.

The cracked yellow skull — it wasn't a mask.

It was hard, like stone. A real skull.

I started to lift the skull before I realized it was attached to a skeleton.

I froze. I was too stunned to let go. The skeleton rose over me. The bones were dry and yellow under the moonlight.

And as I stood there, a strong gust of wind blew through the skeleton's rib bones.

And it moaned.

Now the skeleton rose up. Its cracked skull tilted toward me as if it was looking at me through its empty eye sockets. Its mouth was frozen in a hideous grin. It had only two or thre broken teeth left in its mouth.

Peter bumped up beside me. He tugged my hands off the sides of the skull. Then he uttered a cry as the wind blew through the skeleton's bones and the skeleton moaned again. The leg bones made a cracking sound as they stood taller.

I tried to stagger back, away from the ugly thing.

But it moved with surprising speed.

It grabbed my throat with its hard, bony fingers.

I saw it grab Peter with its other fleshless hand.

We both screamed as the skeleton lifted us off the ground — and heaved us into the open grave.

34

I landed on my hands and knees in wet dirt.

Peter thudded beside me. He rolled onto his side and bumped the wall of the grave.

I gazed up to the top of the hole. I expected the skeleton to appear up there.

I could hear its moaning as the wind blew through its bones. But it didn't follow us down. I couldn't see it.

I pulled myself to my feet. Mud clung to my knees. The dirt beneath us was soft and wet. It smelled sour down there, like spoiled milk.

Beside me, Peter stood and stretched his hands to the top of the grave. He wasn't tall enough to reach it.

He jumped two or three times, trying to grab hold of the ground above the grave. But the mud was too wet. He kept sliding back down to the bottom.

Wiping mud off his hands, he turned to me.

"I . . . think we're trapped down here," he said softly.

Something caught my eyes on the grave bottom. Something glistened in the moonlight. Glistened and *moved.*

I bent down to examine it — and gasped. A clump of worms. Thick as a mop head. Long, wet worms crawling over each other, tangled together. Like a big heap of *moving* spaghetti.

I turned away. And saw more worms poking out of the dirt walls. Dozens of worms dropped down the sides of the grave. Wriggling at my feet in the wet mud.

"I — I hate worms," I stammered. "I have a thing about worms."

"I know," Peter said. "Remember when I put those Gummi Worms in your bed?"

"Shut up, Peter!"

He gazed up at the ground.

"I'll give you a boost," I said. "I'll raise you to the top. After you climb out, you can pull me up."

"Sounds like a plan," he said.

He stepped to the grave wall and turned his back to me, ready for me to boost him up.

But I didn't move.

My eyes were locked on the back of the grave.

Another skull. Pale gray. With deep eye sockets and a jagged-toothed grin. It moved in the darkness. Appeared in front of us, as if out of nowhere.

"Peter —" I whispered.

"Hurry," he said. "I want to get out of this grave."

"No, look," I said, bumping his shoulder. I pointed.

He spun around. He followed my gaze.

Before we could move closer, the skull started to rise.

Moonlight suddenly poured into the grave, and I could see clearly. A man stepped forward. He wore a purple robe with a raised hood. Inside the hood, I could see the grinning skull. A mask.

The skull mask.

"Screem?" The name burst from my throat in a hoarse whisper.

He stood against the far grave wall across from us. The wind rustled his long robe. In the moonlight, I could see the gleam of his purple eyes inside the grinning skull mask.

Screem. How did he suddenly appear? Had he been waiting for us?

"You shouldn't have come."

His old man's voice was muffled inside the mask.

He took a step toward Peter and me.

Above us, the moon disappeared behind clouds again. Darkness fell over the grave.

As my eyes adjusted, I watched Screem reach for the sides of the skull mask. With a hard, swift tug, he pulled off the mask.

His straight white hair fell to his shoulders. I could see beads of sweat on his broad forehead. He rubbed his square white paintbrush beard with his free hand.

His eyes darted back and forth from Peter to me.

"You've made a *terrible* mistake!" he boomed. "You have no business here. You don't know what you are doing."

He took a step toward us. Then another.

Peter and I were trapped against the grave wall.

"Wh-what are you going to *do* with us?" I stammered.

35

Screem moved forward quickly. I heard a loud *squish* sound as he stepped on the glob of worms.

He flattened the worms under the sole of his boot. He kept his eyes straight ahead on Peter and me.

I pressed my back against the dirt wall. No way to escape. We were trapped six feet underground in this narrow hole.

"What are you going to do?" I repeated. My voice cracked as I said the words.

"I warned you," Screem said. "I warned you back at Bella's house."

He held the skull mask tightly in one hand. He reached out his other hand to me.

I tried to squirm away. But there was nowhere to move.

"Turn around," he said. "I'll give you a boost."

I swallowed. My heart was pounding hard. That wasn't what I expected him to say.

A few seconds later, Screem pushed me up to the top of the grave. I scrambled on my hands and knees onto the grass. Then I jumped to my feet.

Peter came crawling out after me. He shook his head, confused. He climbed to his feet.

I turned and saw the moaning skeleton. It stood stiffly beside the grave. Its bony arms dangled at its sides. Its eyeless sockets were trained on Peter and me.

Screem floated up from the grave. His purple robe fluttered in the wind. His white hair blew about his head.

He turned to the skeleton. "Your work is done," he told it.

He raised his hand, and the big jeweled ring glowed on his finger. He pointed the jewel at the skeleton.

The skeleton let out a final moan. Then its bones cracked and broke and fell apart. The bones fell to the grass and crumpled to dust. The dust swirled into the air and blew away.

Screem watched it for a moment. Then he turned to us.

Was he going to raise his ring and zap *us* to dust?

"Give me back the three masks you've found,"

he said. He reached out his hand. "Give them back and get away from here — as fast as you can."

I stared at him. I didn't know what to say. I was too frightened to speak.

"I must hold the masks till dawn," Screem said. "Or you will see evil spread over the world."

A terrifying threat. Bella said that's what would happen if Screem kept the masks.

But I had only one thing on my mind now. And I would never give back the masks till Screem helped us.

"We want our parents!" I cried. "We want our house back. We'll give you the masks when you bring them back."

Screem's purple eyes flashed. He shook his head. "If I don't have those five masks at dawn," he boomed, "you will never see your parents again."

36

The words made my breath catch in my throat.

Screem kept his eyes locked on us. "Bella's evil is so intense, she will stop at nothing," he said.

Huh? BELLA'S evil?

"The magic of the masks is too powerful to be in her hands," he continued. "You do not know who you are working for. You think you are collecting the masks for *good.*"

"I — I don't understand," I stammered. "Are you saying —"

"Bella is evil," Screem said. "She is the one who made your house disappear. Not me. She made your house and parents disappear to trick you into helping her."

My mouth dropped open. Bella told us it was Screem who took away our house. Was Screem telling the truth? Was Bella the evil one?

"This terrible game has to stop," Screem said. "You are not the first people Bella has tortured like this. Some have not been as lucky as you."

The wind ruffled his white hair. His purple robe glowed under the moonlight.

I glanced at Peter. He was shivering. I don't think he was cold. He was shivering from Screem's words.

"You can make it all stop now," Screem continued. "You have to believe me."

Believe. Believe. Believe.

The word stuck in my head.

Should we believe him? *Should* we?

Suddenly, I remembered Bella's warning as we were leaving her house.

Screem is the best liar on earth.

It's almost impossible not *to believe him.*

Whatever you do, do not believe what he tells you. Do not fall for his lies.

"Don't believe him," I whispered to Peter.

I turned to Screem. "Bella warned us you are a liar," I said.

Screem shook the skull mask in his fist. "Listen to me carefully," he said. "Her real name isn't Bella. It's *Belladonna.* Do you know what that is?"

I repeated the name in my mind. "I've heard of it," I said.

"Belladonna," Screem said. "Sometimes it's called deadly nightshade. It's a poison. *She* is a poison."

I knew he was lying.

I pressed my hands against my waist. "If you

are on the side of good," I said, "why did you make it so dangerous for Peter and me to take the masks?"

"Yeah," Peter said. He took a few steps toward Screem. "You tried to kill us each time. So why should we believe that you are on the side of good?"

"You were working for Belladonna," Screem replied. "I couldn't just let you walk away with the masks. I had to try to stop you. I had no choice."

"You're lying to us," Peter said. He raised his arms in a karate position.

"I don't care what you think," Screem said. "If you don't want to believe the truth, that's fine with me."

He stretched out a hand and moved toward us rapidly. "Just give me the three masks. *Now!*"

I stumbled back. But Peter held his ground.

Screem dove forward, his hand outstretched to tear the masks off our faces.

Peter uttered a cry. He leaped sideways into the air — and tried to land a two-footed karate kick to Screem's knees.

Peter missed.

His shoes kicked at nothing but air.

Screem grabbed Peter by the ankles.

He tugged him hard. Lost his balance — and they both toppled into the open grave.

37

My heart thudding in my chest, I stared toward the open grave. I wanted to hurry to the side of the grave. But I froze. My legs wouldn't carry me.

I held my breath and listened.

Silence.

Even the wind had stopped. The trees over the old graveyard stood perfectly still.

I listened for Peter's screams. Or the sounds of a fight. Or someone scraping and scrabbling to climb out.

But no.

Not a sound.

The silence felt so loud, I pressed my hands over my ears.

"Peter?"

Finally, I forced myself forward. I took a step toward the grave.

"Peter?"

Silence.

I lowered my hands to my sides. I had them balled into tight, tense fists.

I took another step toward the grave.

"Peter? Can you hear me?"

I took a deep breath and held it. Then I leaned over the grave and peered down.

"No. Oh, no," I murmured.

The grave was empty.

38

I dropped to my knees in the wet dirt. A shudder made my whole body shake.

"Peter? Where are you?" I called in a trembling voice.

I stared down into the empty grave. "Impossible," I muttered.

Unless Screem used his magic to carry them both away somewhere?

Unless Screem used the same magic on Peter that he used to make our parents disappear?

I leaned down into the grave and shouted: "Peter? Are you there? Please — answer me!"

No reply.

I leaned farther into the grave. "Peter?"

And then I let out a gasp as the soft mud gave way beneath me. I fell fast. And landed on my stomach on the floor of the grave.

"Ohhhhh," I groaned as I realized I'd landed on top of the pile of worms. "Noooo."

I jumped up quickly.

"Peter? Where are you?" My voice rang hollow against the dirt sides.

I brushed fat worms off the front of my clothes.

"Peter? Can you hear me?"

Keeping my hand on the grave wall, I began to move. I took tiny steps along the side of the hole. I traced my hand on the dirt. I needed something to hold on to.

Above me, the moon slid out from behind the clouds once again. Pale yellow light washed over the grave.

And in the light, I saw an opening at the far end. Like a low doorway cut into the grave wall.

I hurried across the dirt. I stopped a few inches away. Moonlight helped me see inside the opening.

I saw a tunnel. A narrow tunnel leading straight ahead to solid blackness.

So that's where they vanished. Into this tunnel cut into the graveside.

Again, I cupped my hand around my mouth and shouted my brother's name.

I heard my voice echo down the tunnel. The tunnel was deep and straight.

I moved into the opening. And stopped. I struggled to catch my breath.

Screem had dragged Peter into this tunnel. There was nowhere else they could be.

I had to go after him.

I ducked my head. I took a shaky step into the tunnel opening.

And stopped.

I heard the heavy thud of shoes on dirt. Running footsteps.

In the dim light, I saw Screem. Racing toward me through the tunnel, hands outstretched.

"Noooooo!" I opened my mouth in a scream.

Nowhere to run.

Screem had me trapped down in the grave. Did he plan to pull me into the long, dark tunnel, too?

39

I tensed my muscles. How could I fight him?

Then he came thundering into the moonlight — and I gasped.

"Peter?"

It wasn't Screem. It was my brother. Still wearing the mummy mask. The belt of his karate uniform dragging on the dirt.

He ran up to me, breathing hard. He raised both hands. A mask dangled from each hand.

I stared in shock. Peter had the skull mask and the alien pig mask.

"Did you . . . did you grab those from Screem?" I demanded.

He nodded.

"How did you do it?" I cried. "How did you take them away from Screem?"

I gazed into the tunnel. "Where *is* Screem?"

Peter shook his head. "No time," he whispered. I could barely hear him through the mummy mask. "Let's go."

I realized we had all five masks. Peter had three, and I was wearing two.

"Is Screem coming after us?" I asked.

Peter motioned frantically with both hands. "No time." His voice was a hoarse whisper.

He pushed me to the edge of the grave. Then he bent and gave me a boost.

I scrambled up to the ground. Then I turned and pulled him out of the grave.

I glanced down. Where was Screem?

I was dying for Peter to explain. But he took off, running hard through the paths between the gravestones. He waved for me to follow.

My shoes slipped and slid on flat dead leaves as I ran to catch up. The darkness was lifting. The sky had brightened from black to violet. And I could see a broad stripe of red sunlight rising low through the trees.

"Almost dawn," I murmured.

At the edge of the graveyard, we came to a sharp stop. The twin beams of car headlights swept down the street. Peter and I ducked behind a fat tree trunk and waited for the car to pass.

When it turned a corner, we took off running again. Peter didn't say a word, but I knew where he was heading. Back to Bella's house.

We had all five masks. Now it was her turn to help us. We needed her to use the magic of the masks to return our parents and our house.

But I felt a shudder of fear as I watched the red stripe on the horizon rise. The sky had brightened to gray.

Were we too late?

We cut through front yards, keeping in the shadows of trees and tall hedges. When we passed the empty lot where our house used to stand, I stopped.

A sob escaped my throat. I wanted to cry and scream and shake my fists and roar at the sky.

I stared at the carpet of tall grass and weeds. No sign that a house had ever been there.

How could this happen to our parents? What if we really were too late?

A light went on in the house next door. Another car rumbled past on the street behind me.

No time to waste. Dawn was arriving.

I darted around a bike lying on its side in the next driveway. I caught up with Peter at the corner. We tore across the street and kept running.

Peter held the masks out at his sides as he ran. A short while later, the tall hedges in front of Bella's house came into view.

We cut through the opening in the hedges and turned up the driveway. Our shoes sent the gravel flying.

We stopped, both breathing hard, on the front stoop. I raised my hand to ring the doorbell — then stopped.

"Look. The door is open a crack," I said.

Beneath the mummy mask, Peter was panting hard. He pushed the door open a little farther.

I poked my head into the front entryway. "Bella?" My voice was muffled under the two masks.

I tried again. "Bella?" This time I shouted.

No reply.

I led the way into the house. I trotted into the front room. Peter hurried close behind me.

"Bella?" I shouted. "We're back. Are we too late?"

Silence.

I heard a clock ticking. As loud as drumbeats in the heavy silence.

"We have the five masks!" I called. "We have them all."

I gazed around the front room. Then I ran to the library in the back, calling her name.

No sign of her.

I led the way down the back hall, which led to the kitchen. Empty. A red sun was just rising in the kitchen window.

I screamed her name at the top of my lungs.

No answer.

Finally, I turned to Peter. "What are we going to do? She isn't here. She's *gone*."

40

"She'll be here," Peter whispered, so low I could barely hear him. "She *has* to be here."

And then I heard a rustling sound. Padding footsteps.

I turned to see Bella coming down the front stairway. Her long dress trailed behind her. She swept back her hair, and a broad smile crossed her face as she saw us.

"You're here!" she cried. "I'm sorry. I had given up hope."

She practically flew down the stairs. Her smile stayed frozen on her face. Her eyes glowed with excitement.

She ran into the kitchen and rushed up to Peter and me with her hands outstretched. "You have all five?"

"Yes," I said. "Are we in time? We brought you the five masks and —"

Her hands flew up in the air. "You did it! I'm

so proud of you!" she cried. "Hand them to me. Quickly."

She glanced out the kitchen window. The sun was a red ball, still low behind the trees.

"It's almost dawn," she said. "Hurry. Take off the masks. Hand them to me — now!"

"You said — you said you couldn't touch them," I said.

She raised her hands. She was wearing long black gloves. "Quick. Hand them to me."

I grabbed the snow wolf mask and started to tug up on its sides. It stuck to the mask beneath it. I couldn't get it to slide.

I gave a harder tug — then stopped.

I turned to Peter. To my surprise, he wasn't moving. He stood staring at Bella through the mummy mask. He held the other two masks down at his sides.

"Hurry," Bella urged. She leaned over him. "What's wrong with you? Hand me those masks."

Peter didn't move. He kept his hands down stiffly at his sides. He stared out at Bella.

She made a wild grab for the alien pig mask.

Peter swung his body around to keep it safe in his hand.

"Give them to me!" Bella screamed. Her face turned bright red. "It's almost dawn. Give them to me. Do I have to rip that mask off your head, you little punk?"

I gasped, startled that Bella was acting so furious and out of control.

"You punk! You creep! You disgusting little worm!" Bella shrieked at my brother. "Give me those masks!"

She made another frantic grab. Missed. Her hand wrapped around the belt of his karate uniform.

Peter tugged himself free. He didn't say a word. Just stood there stiffly, in silence, holding the masks out of Bella's reach.

A stripe of yellow sunlight spread across the floor.

"Peter," I said softly. "What are you doing? Why —"

And then he tucked the two masks under his arm. Without a word, he reached both hands to the bottom of the mummy mask.

With one hard tug, he pulled the mummy mask off his face.

"NOOOO!" Bella and I both shrieked at the same time.

My mouth hung open. My eyes bulged. It took a while for my brain to realize — it wasn't Peter standing next to me.

It was Screem!

41

Screem's white hair fell over his forehead. He brushed it back with one sleeve. He tucked the mummy mask under his arm with the other two masks. Then he grinned at Bella.

"Surprise, Belladonna!" he cried. "I have the masks, and I've come back to *destroy* you!"

She gaped at him in horror. Her face was as pale as flour. Her chin trembled.

Above his square beard, Screem's grin grew wider. "I forgot. You don't like surprise guests — do you!" he boomed.

"I — I —" Bella seemed too upset to speak. "The boy —" she choked out.

"He believed me," Screem replied. "The boy realized I was telling the truth. So down in my tunnel in the graveyard, he and I traded places."

"I . . . told him you were a liar," Bella said. She kept clenching and unclenching her gloved fists.

"It wasn't hard to make the boy see who the *real* liar is," Screem said.

Screem turned suddenly. Without warning, he grabbed my shoulders.

I gasped. "What are you *doing*?" I cried.

His hands moved to the masks over my face. Carefully, he slid them off one by one.

Now he grasped all five masks in his hands.

"The masks are mine," Screem said. "Belladonna, the world is safe from your evil for another year."

She scowled at me. Her eyes flamed with rage. "Monica, your brother *betrayed* me. Do you think I won't punish you both?"

Screem stepped in front of me. "You won't do any punishing this year," he told her. "Did you really think you could confuse me by sending two *children* this time? You're a bigger loser than I thought."

"AAAAGGGGGGH!"

Belladonna opened her mouth in a scream of fury. A wild animal cry.

She leaped at Screem. Lowered her shoulder and shoved him back on the kitchen counter.

Then with another angry cry, she grabbed the masks from Screem's hands.

He bounced up from the counter. He spread his arms like an attacking bear. He flung himself at Belladonna.

The masks fell from her hands.

They both dove for them at once.

"Mine! Mine! Mine!" she kept screeching.

But Screem came up with the masks.

As he tried to tuck them under the white karate uniform, Belladonna wrapped her arms around his middle. She struggled to wrestle him to the floor.

Screem staggered back, off balance.

"Mine! Mine! Mine!" Belladonna repeated.

They both dropped to the floor, wrestling, struggling, scratching at each other. They groaned and grunted and shouted as they fought.

They rolled across the kitchen floor. Toward the big window. Into a patch of morning sunlight.

Yes. The sun was high in the sky now.

And as Screem and Belladonna rolled into the bright sunlight, I saw a flash of white light.

Blinding white light. Like a powerful explosion.

I shut my eyes.

I could still see the light on my eyelids.

And when I finally opened my eyes, the two of them were gone. And the masks had vanished with them.

Screem and Belladonna — both disappeared into the sunlight. Their screams still rang in my ears.

I felt dazed. I struggled to clear my mind, to think straight. And as I did, a wave of cold fear ran down my body.

And a terrifying question pushed its way into my mind:

Where is Peter?

What became of my brother?

Would I ever see him again? Or had he vanished like Screem . . . like Belladonna? Like our parents?

42

I wrapped my arms around myself. I felt cold despite the warm sunlight washing into the kitchen.

The silence rang in my ears, a hollow sound. And then I jumped when I heard the thud of footsteps. In the front hall.

I turned — and saw the purple robe.

Screem? Had he returned?

No. Peter grinned at me. He stepped into the kitchen and did a funny tap dance. "Tah-DAH!"

"Peter? That robe —" I uttered. "You —"

"Fits me perfectly," he said. "But I don't think I'll wear it to school."

"How — how can you stand there making jokes?" I stammered.

He shrugged. "Halloween is over, right? And we're alive."

I rushed up to him. I had a million questions. "Where were you? Why didn't you come back here with Screem?"

"He told me not to show myself until it was bright sunshine," Peter answered. "He said it would all be over by then. And we'd be safe."

"Oh, wow. Oh, wow." I was so happy to see him, I nearly hugged him.

"Peter, it's morning," I said. I grabbed him by the shoulders. "Mom and Dad. They must be out of their minds worrying about us. They probably have the police out looking for us."

Peter's smile faded. "*If* they're back," he said softly.

His words sent a chill down my back. "Halloween is over," I said. "Belladonna and Screem are gone. That means everything is back to normal. Everything . . ."

I sighed. "Our house *has* to be back, Peter," I cried. "Mom and Dad *have* to be back."

We didn't say another word. We ran down the hall and out the front door. We didn't even bother to close the door behind us.

Our shoes thudded down the gravel driveway, past the tall hedges to the street. Cars rolled past. Two little kids were in the yard across the street, jumping up and down in a pile of dead leaves.

A normal Saturday morning.

Yes. Normal. A woman opened her front door and let her dog run out. A white mail truck turned the corner. The two little kids waved to it.

Normal.

We turned the corner onto our block. We ran past the empty field, past two houses.

I couldn't see our house. Trees stood in the way.

My heart was pounding so hard, I could barely breathe. Running was too slow. I wanted to leap into the air and *fly* to our house.

Finally, we were there. Finally, we could see. . . .

"OH, NOOOOOO!" I wailed.

Behind me, I heard Peter utter a scream. "Noooooo."

Still an empty field. I stared up at the ragged lawn. Nothing but tall grass and weeds.

No house. No parents.

My whole body sagged. My knees folded. I dropped to the wet ground.

Gone. Everything. Still gone.

43

"What are we going to do? What are we going to do?"

Peter kept repeating the same words over and over. Each time his voice got more shrill.

He stood staring up to where the house should be. His hands were pressed tightly to the sides of his face.

"Halloween is over," he said. "Everything is supposed to be back to normal. Everything . . ." His voice trailed off.

My brain was spinning. This couldn't be happening.

Bella and Screem were gone. The world should be back to normal.

Think, Monica. . . . Think!

I tugged Peter's arm. "Come with me," I said. "I think I just figured out how to bring back Mom and Dad."

He held back. "Where are we going?" he asked.

"Back to Bella's house," I said.

* * *

"Anyone home?" I called. Peter and I huddled tensely in the front hallway.

No answer.

I peered into the living room. No one there. Nothing changed. Except for the bright golden sunlight pouring through the front window.

"Bella and Screem are totally gone," Peter said. "But this house is creepy even when it's empty. It's like the air is haunted or something."

I nodded. "Don't think about it," I said in a whisper. "Follow me. We have to find *The Hallows Book*."

We hurried through the living room to the library at the back. Shelves were still overturned. We stepped over the books scattered on the floor.

"Why do you want that old book?" Peter asked.

"I have an idea," I told him.

It didn't take long to find it. It was tucked onto a small bottom shelf. But it was so big, it stuck out into the room.

The old book weighed a ton. Peter helped me carry it to the long table in the center of the room. Dust flew up when we dropped it to the table.

"Help me turn it over," I said. "I want to start at the back."

The heavy cover was stained and bumpy. One of the corners was torn away.

It took us a while to get a good grip. Then we flipped the book onto its front.

I leaned over the table and opened the back cover. The book smelled musty, like the back of an old closet. I held my nose to keep from sneezing.

Then I lifted the pages until I found the end of the book.

"Peter, listen to this," I said. And I read the last paragraphs out loud:

"Bella and Screem vanished in the sunlight. Peter and Monica ran home. But their home was not returned.

"They had saved the world from Belladonna's evil. But their parents were gone. And the two kids were doomed to live without them."

Peter shook his head sadly. "It's all there," he said. His voice cracked. "It's in the book. Mom and Dad are gone."

"Maybe not," I said. "Maybe I can change everything."

I found a pen on the floor. I picked it up and leaned over *The Hallows Book*. My hand started to tremble. But I steadied it and lowered it to the page.

I crossed out the last lines of the story, the words I had read to Peter. And then the marking pen scratched over the rough paper as I wrote in a new ending. . . .

The house returned. The parents were okay. It was Halloween night again. And Monica and Peter returned home with their trick-or-treat bags full.

They forgot everything that had happened to them. Their horrifying memories were wiped clean. And they returned happily to their normal lives.

I let out a long sigh. Then I read my new ending to Peter. "What do you think?" I asked.

He stared hard at me. "I don't know," he said finally. "Do you really think that will work?"

44

I blinked. And let out a cry.

Sudden darkness fell over the room.

It took a few seconds for me to realize why the sunlight had disappeared. I rushed to the front window and gazed out. The half-moon stood high in the black sky. It was night again.

"Peter — let's go," I said.

We ran out of the dark house. I gasped when Peter stepped into the light. He was dressed in his white karate uniform again. And he held his bulging trick-or-treat bag tightly in one fist.

I glanced up at the moon. "It must be late," I said.

Peter turned to the enormous house behind us. "Whose house is this?" he asked. "What are we doing here?"

I turned to follow his gaze. "I — I don't remember," I said.

We ran home. We passed a few trick-or-treaters. Mostly older kids who could stay out late. A big yellow-orange jack-o'-lantern grinned at us from a front stoop as we followed the sidewalk to our block.

All the lights were on in our house. The front door opened as Peter and I ran up the middle of the lawn. Mom and Dad were both waiting at the door.

"We were a little worried," Mom said. "You usually don't stay out this late."

"We hit a few more houses," I said. I rolled my eyes. "Peter's idea — not mine."

He raised his trick-or-treat bag. "Check it out."

Dad reached for the bag. "You *are* going to share this year — right?"

"Yeah. Right," Peter said. He pulled the bag out of Dad's reach and trotted up the stairs.

I followed him up to his room. We always dump our candy on the floor, divide it up, and make trades.

Peter stepped into the center of the room. He raised his big trick-or-treat bag over his head and turned it upside down.

A few pieces of candy came falling out. But then . . . then . . .

. . . Five ugly rubber masks toppled out of the bag. They hit the floor and all landed faceup.

I stepped back. I couldn't take my eyes off them. They were all so horrible looking.

"Peter — what are those? Wh-where did you get them?" I stammered.

He shrugged. "I . . . don't know."

The five masks appeared to gaze up at me. And at that moment, it all came back to me.

"Noooooo!" I screamed as the masks opened their gaping mouths wide — and began to laugh.

WELCOME BACK TO THE HALL OF HORRORS

Well, Monica, your Halloween story is a real SCREAM, no matter how you spell it.

Are you sure that story has been repeating itself for one hundred years? You don't look a day over ninety-eight!

Ha-ha. I know. I know. You're only twelve. I like to have my little joke. You know the old rhyme — a laugh a day keeps the werewolves away.

So try laughing on your way out. Maybe you'll be luckier than my last visitor.

Thank you for bringing your story to me. I am the Story-Keeper. And I will keep your story here in the Hall of Horrors where it belongs.

And now, we have a new guest. Come right in, young man.

What is your name? Matt Krinsky?

You appear so tired, Matt. Why are you staggering like that? You look *dead on your feet.*

Has anyone told you you look like a *zombie*?

Come in. Come in. Stagger this way. There's plenty of room in the Hall of Horrors. You know. . . . There's Always Room for One More Scream.

Ready for More?

Here's another tale from the Hall of Horrors:

WHY I QUIT ZOMBIE SCHOOL

"YOWWWWWWWWW!"

That's me, Jack Harmon, screaming my head off. I was on the school bus, heading home, howling in pain. As usual.

You would scream, too, if Mick Owens had you in an armlock. Mick shoved my arm up behind me till I heard my bones and muscles snap and pop.

"YOWWWWWWW!" I repeated.

Nothing new here. Big Mick and his friend Darryl "The Hammer" Oliva like to beat me up, tease and torture me on the bus every afternoon.

Last week, our sixth-grade teacher, Miss Harris, had a long, serious talk in class about bullying. I guess Mick and Darryl were out that day.

Otherwise, they would know that bullying is bad.

Why do they do it? Because I'm smaller than them? Because I'm a skinny little guy who looks like a third-grader? Because I scream easily?

No.

These two super-hulks like to get up in my face because it's FUN.

About the Author

R.L. Stine's books are read all over the world. So far, his books have sold more than 300 million copies, making him one of the most popular children's authors in history. Besides Goosebumps, R.L. Stine has written the teen series Fear Street and the funny series Rotten School, as well as the Mostly Ghostly series, The Nightmare Room series, and the two-book thriller *Dangerous Girls*. R.L. Stine lives in New York with his wife, Jane, and Minnie, his King Charles spaniel. You can learn more about him at www.RLStine.com.

Goosebumps
HorrorLand
TM

AN ALL-NEW, ALL-TERRIFYING SERIES FROM THE MASTER OF FRIGHT!
Goosebumps
HorrorLand
REVENGE OF THE LIVING DUMMY
R.L. STINE
SCHOLASTIC

Goosebumps
HorrorLand
CREEP FROM THE DEEP
R.L. STINE
SCHOLASTIC

Goosebumps
HorrorLand
MONSTER BLOOD FOR BREAKFAST!
R.L. STINE
SCHOLASTIC

Goosebumps
HorrorLand
THE SCREAM OF THE HAUNTED MASK
R.L. STINE
SCHOLASTIC

Goosebumps
HorrorLand
DR. MANIAC VS. ROBBY SCHWARTZ
R.L. STINE
SCHOLASTIC

Goosebumps
HorrorLand
WHO'S YOUR MUMMY?
R.L. STINE
SCHOLASTIC

Goosebumps
HorrorLand
MY FRIENDS CALL ME MONSTER
R.L. STINE
SCHOLASTIC

Goosebumps
HorrorLand
SAY CHEESE – AND DIE SCREAMING!
R.L. STINE
SCHOLASTIC

Goosebumps
HorrorLand
WELCOME TO CAMP SLITHER
R.L. STINE
SCHOLASTIC

R. L. Stine's Fright Fest!

Now with Splat Stats and More!

Read them all!

SCHOLASTIC

www.scholastic.com/goosebumps

GBCL21